Praise for Joseph L.S. Terrell's
Harrison Weaver Mysteries

Undertow of Vengeance, Joseph Terrell's fourth thriller in the Harrison Weaver crime writer series, and set in North Carolina's Outer Banks, is a knockout. With the deadpan savvy delivery of Humphrey Bogart as Sam Spade and the clipped declarative sentences of Dashiell Hammett, this volume, like its predecessors, reaches out in the very first sentence, grabs you by the lapels, and never lets up.
—Joseph Bathanti, former North Carolina Poet Laureate

Smooth writing from an eloquent storyteller goes down like fine scotch. *Undertow of Vengeance* is a keeper.
—Maggie Toussaint, Author, Cleopatra Jones Mysteries

"Every once in a while I'll pick up a book and from the first sentence, I'm engaged. Written with an extraordinary eye for detail yet in the sparse language of the journalist he once was, Terrell's novel is filled with wonderful dialogue, believable characters and just enough plot twists to keep the reader turning pages."
—Kip Tabb, Freelance Writer, former Ed. *North Beach Sun*

"Joe Terrell gets the Outer Banks just right, from crashing surf to the sordid crimes behind the tourism façade, to a thoughtful sleuth who can throw a punch and make a mean sweet tea."
—David Healey, Author, *The House That Went Down With The Ship*

"A smart, savvy combination of who-done-it and police procedural."
—Kathryn R. Wall, Author, the Bay Tanner Mysteries

**Books by
Joseph L.S. Terrell**

Harrison Weaver Mysteries

TIDE OF DARKNESS
OVERWASH OF EVIL
NOT OUR KIND OF KILLING
UNDERTOW OF VENGEANCE
DEAD RIGHT RETURNING
THE LAST BLUE NOON IN MAY

Jonathan Clayton Novels

THE OTHER SIDE OF SILENCE
LEARNING TO SLOW DANCE

Stand Alones

A TIME OF MUSIC, A TIME OF MAGIC

A NEUROTIC'S GUIDE TO SANE LIVING

THE SERPENTINE FLOWER

THE LAST BLUE NOON IN MAY

A HARRISON WEAVER MYSTERY

JOSEPH L.S. TERRELL

BellaRosaBooks

BellaRosaBooks

THE LAST BLUE NOON IN MAY
ISBN 978-1-62268-125-9

First Printed: June 2017

Library of Congress Control Number: 2017943765

Also available as e-book: ISBN 978-1-62268-126-6

Printed in the United States of America on acid-free paper.

Cover photograph and design by Roo Harris.
Author photograph by Richard Betrand - Paris.

Book design by Bella Rosa Books

10   9   8   7   6   5   4   3   2   1

Once again, this book is dedicated with love to Veronica, who brings joy and zest into my life.

Acknowledgments

Thanks to former FBI Agent Larry Likar for his insight into serial killers and other crimes, and to author Gwen Hunter for help as always on forensic matters. Real appreciation to manuscript readers Cathy Kelly and Veronica Moschetti Reich for their catches and suggestions that made the story better. A special debt of gratitude for the expert and professional editing of Beth Terrell, a tough but kind taskmaster, who always improves a work of fiction. And I want to thank Gale Anne Friedel, who encouraged me to tell more about the fictional character Deputy Odell Wright in a story. Also, Roo Harris for his creativity and patience in once again furnishing a cover design for one of my books. Thanks, too, for the support of independent bookstore owners Jamie Hope Anderson of Duck's Cottage and Downtown Books, and to Bill Rickman of Island Bookstores, and Meaghan, who oversees book signings. As always, my deepest gratitude to my publisher, Rod Hunter of Bella Rosa Books, for his continuing faith in me as a writer.

—JLST

Author's Note:

This is a work of fiction, and while most of the place names at the Outer Banks are real, the main characters in this story exist only in the author's imagination, and bear no resemblance to persons living or dead. This is especially true of the character known in this story as the "Bear Woman." Readers familiar with North Carolina's Outer Banks will recognize that, as usual, I have used the historic Dare County Courthouse as it was used years ago to house the sheriff's and other offices.

–*JLST*

THE LAST BLUE
NOON IN MAY

Chapter One

At first, I assumed Chief Deputy Odell Wright was deep in thought as he sat alone in the windowless interrogation room at the sheriff's office. With his back to me, he pored over a thick sheaf of papers from a case file. The file did not look like a new one. It was too dog-eared and some of the pages appeared yellowed with age, including a few faded newspaper articles pushed to one side.

But something about his overall posture told me there was more to it than simple contemplation. His shoulders, usually so broad and erect, were slumped and rounded. He rubbed the palm of one hand across his close-cropped black hair, which had only the beginnings along his temples of silvery gray. Then he propped his chin up with the same palm. He seemed to lack the stamina or the will to hold his head up.

I stood in the open doorway, ready to speak to him. But I decided not to. I stayed perfectly still. Maybe it was my imagination but I sensed he gave the tiniest shake of his head in dismay as he turned page after page of the report in front of him.

Quietly, I stepped fully back into the hallway. A few feet from the door to the sheriff's office, I saw Mabel. She had stopped and watched me move away from the interrogation room. A tired smile softened her face.

Mabel has been with the sheriff's department maybe a hundred years. Well, certainly not that long, although to hear her tell it, it's been about that. She worked first for the long-time Sheriff Claxton, starting there when she was a relatively young woman. Difficult to think of Mabel ever being young. After Sheriff Claxton's death several years ago, she stayed on and serves Sheriff Eugene Albright with the same dedication.

I can't imagine the sheriff's office without Mabel. Today she wore one of her usual loose-fitting tops in muted green and brown and a full skirt that came down to mid-calf. Her shoes were the comfortable looking soft black ones that ran over a bit on the side.

She eyed me and remained still. I approached her and stood close. Tilting my head back toward the interrogation room, I said, "He okay?"

Mabel gave the slightest little nod. "It's May fourth," she said softly.

I knew there was a quizzical cast to my face, an eyebrow raised. Taking my cue from her, I lowered my voice. "Yes?"

She turned one palm toward her small office, which was next to the sheriff's. When I followed her in, she moved behind her desk and eased herself into the large, leatherette upholstered, high-back chair. The chair was a castoff of one the sheriff had used before getting an even fancier one. Without speaking she pointed to one of the straight chairs in front of her desk, and I took it. A small green lamp on her desk glowed softly, illuminating a few prints on the wall. One was by local artist James Melvin of a peaceful front porch scene with two rocking chairs overlooking the beach and the ocean. Behind her was a large framed map of Dare County and much of the Outer Banks. Her little office looked homier than anything else in the sheriff's office there in downtown Manteo's courthouse.

I'm not sure why, but I almost whispered when I queried, "May fourth?"

She had the softest, kindest expression around her eyes. "Yes. Every May fourth he goes over that file from beginning to end, page by page."

I leaned forward so I could catch all of her words.

Mabel said, "May fourth is the anniversary of the day his little sister disappeared. She was nine years old. This is the twenty-first—no, the twenty-second—anniversary of her disappearance. Her abduction, it had to be. And never any trace. Not the slightest."

I sank back in my chair, shaking my head. I was stunned. This was the first I knew about that, and I had been acquainted with Odell Wright for almost five years now. Maybe we were not close, but with an effective and smooth enough working relationship from time to time, and I certainly held him in high regard as a lawman and human being. He was always gracious and blessed with a wry sense of humor, and that was how I knew him. Yet, I didn't have any idea about this tragedy that obviously plagued him.

Her voice soft, Mabel said, "Odell has never gotten over it. Neither did his parents. His mother's dead now. I think the tragedy just broke her heart and her spirit to live. His daddy's still alive but I don't think he's in good health."

Looking over Mabel's gray head to something a thousand yards into the distance, I said, "We never really know what ghosts other people wrestle with, do we?"

Mabel said, "Odell was only about eighteen or nineteen when this happened. But he got real involved with Sheriff Claxton and the others trying to find her, find out what happened. He was here at the courthouse every day, and with the search parties that were organized. He practically lived here, it seemed like." She took a deep breath, glanced down at her hands, and then back up into my face. "It was because of this, I know, that made Odell decide he wanted to be a lawman."

"He's never given up on it? Her disappearance?"

"No. Not at all." She compressed her lips for an instant.

"Of course, he doesn't say anything about it much anymore but I know it still is with him, and every May on this date he gets that file and reads every word in it. Takes him two hours or more. No one bothers him."

"So sad," I said. "Never, ever any leads? Not the slightest? No suspects? Nothing?" Then I added softly, hating to ask it: "Her body . . . her body never found?"

She shook her head. "Never any trace of her. As for suspects, a couple of people were questioned. People that the sheriff knew had . . . well, had something of a reputation . . . but they all had alibis and nothing panned out." Two little wrinkles creased her brow. "It was such a pretty day, too. I remember that because the very next day a front came in and it turned real chilly and rainy. But still a search party—lots of volunteers, in raincoats and ponchos—searched and searched. All along the water, the woods over on what's now Festival Park, all around. White people and black. Lots of folks. It was about the first time something like this had ever happened."

Then, obviously remembering something about the little girl, she permitted herself the slightest trace of a smile. "Luanne was such a cute young thing, too. Very friendly. Came down here to the waterfront lots of afternoons. Always smiling and sort of singing to herself. Whistled tunes a lot too."

Then Mabel's eyes focused on a slip of paper near her phone. "Oh, I've got to get this message to the sheriff."

I took that as a signal to leave, and I stood, fingers of one hand resting on the edge of her desk. "Thank you for telling me that," I said quietly. "I had no idea."

Mabel gave one of her kindly smiles and pushed herself up from her chair, taking the slip of paper in one hand. She sighed deeply and made her way around her desk. She's given up on dieting, she says, and vows she'll not complain about her knees and hips aching. She doesn't have to complain. It's easy to see the pain in the way she moves. But her determined smile is always there and except for the look in her eyes and the way she clenches he jaw muscles when she walks, you'd never know she was hurting.

I stepped out into the hall just ahead of her, then moved aside to let her pass. She nodded at me, smiled, and headed to the sheriff's office with the slip of paper in her hand.

Quietly, I retraced my passage back toward the interrogation room. I paused there a moment. Odell Wright sat in the same position but stared off into the distance as if he weren't closeted in that tiny room. It was as if he could see back into the past, to relive those years of long ago; as if, by some means, he could conjure up those last hours when his sister disappeared, and bring her back again.

Chapter Two

Maybe he sensed my standing there in the hall. Odell turned and looked at me. He rose, with the barest trace of a sad smile. He nodded.

I didn't know whether to say anything or not. True to form, though, I spoke. I didn't have to try for feeling; it was there. "Odell, I didn't know anything about your sister, not until just a few minutes ago when Mabel told me." I shook my head. "I'm so sorry . . . I had no idea . . ."

He took a tentative short step toward me. His dark brown eyes took in my face. "It was a long time ago. I wouldn't expect you to know." He stood straight now, his broad shoulders squared away as I usually saw him. He reached behind him and put his right hand lightly on the file, which he had reassembled and placed in the folder. The file was maybe two inches thick.

I was silent, watching.

He said, "I keep going over this file, time and time again. I've read every word in it probably a thousand times . . . and added a few notes of my own." That sad smile flickered for a moment. "I guess I keep hoping I see something I hadn't seen before." He shook his head.

I stood there waiting.

He turned back to the table and picked up the file. He held it close. I could tell he wanted to say something else. He stared down at the file, then raised his head toward me again. "Actually, I'm glad you happened to come by today. I've been thinking that maybe . . . if you're not too busy . . . if maybe you could take a look at the file. Maybe, just maybe, you'll see something I've been missing all these years." He gave a slight shrug as if he thought he might be asking too much. "It'd be sort of an imposition on you, and I probably shouldn't have even mentioned it . . . but . . ."

I tried a reassuring smile. "No problem at all, Odell. I'd be honored to go over the file." I gave a self-deprecating half-chuckle and the barest of a shrug. "Not that I think I might see something that, you know, sparks something. Just the same, I'd deem it a real honor that you'd like for me to go over the file."

He took another short step toward me so that we stood only about two feet from each other. Holding the file in both hands now, he offered it to me. "It's a real old file, and the sheriff won't mind if you take it with you—say, overnight or something—and we'll get together when it's convenient for you."

I took the file and tucked it under my arm. "I'll be careful with it, Odell." I managed a bit more of a smile. "Actually, I'm in-between assignments now so I'll read it this afternoon and tonight. "Maybe meet tomorrow? Go over the file and some of the background."

For the first time, Odell got a real smile. "Back here, at say noon tomorrow?"

"You've got to eat lunch. How about Darrell's at twelve?"

"That would be great," he said.

I extended my hand and we shook. He shook almost enthusiastically.

I turned to leave. "But, Odell, don't expect me to come up with anything that you haven't seen many times before."

"I understand," he said, "and thank you so much."

As I took the stairs down to the first floor, I knew there was virtually no chance I would see anything revealing in the file, but I wished fervently that there would be some way I could help Odell solve this decades-old tragedy.

My name is Harrison Weaver and I'm a crime writer. After a number of years in the Washington area, I made my home on North Carolina's Outer Banks, the tough, sinewy arm of barrier islands that more or less protect mainland North Carolina from the Atlantic Ocean. The elbow of the arm pokes out to sea at Cape Hatteras. To the north there's Kitty Hawk, Southern Shores and Duck; at the south of the arm, Ocracoke Island. Manteo, the county seat of Dare County, is on Roanoke Island, just to the west of the Outer Banks islands.

Because of my writing, I spend a lot of time hanging around the courthouse. Well, to tell the truth, that's not the only reason I find myself at the old courthouse. Ellen Pedersen works there. Everyone, including me, calls her Elly. She works in the Register of Deeds office. Yes, she's my sweetheart. I met her shortly after I moved to the Outer Banks. And now more and more people seem to accept us as "going steady," a description we might use if we were of a different generation.

We're both widowed. She lost her young husband several years ago. She has a five-year-old son named Martin, who has come around enough to speak to me occasionally. My wife died before I left the Washington area. I'm just now getting to the point that I can say simply she died—rather than the truth, that she killed herself with pills.

After going down the stairs to leave the courthouse that May morning, I approached the Register of Deeds' office near the front door. Inside the office, Elly had her back to me, hefting one of the large record books back into a slot. She had her hair pinned up but, as usual, one or two strands of her dark brown hair escaped and graced the whiteness of her neck. I always liked to look at that.

One of her colleagues, Janet, saw me and said, "Hello,

Mr. Weaver." Then, in her singsong voice, said, "Elly, you've got a special visitor."

Elly smiled and turned toward me. I nodded and returned her smile. Maybe something was missing from my smile because she looked at me and said, "Are you all right?"

"Oh, yes. Fine," I said.

She tilted her head at me, questioning.

I moved to one end of the counter. She followed me. Quietly I said, "I was just upstairs. Saw Odell going over an old file." I know I frowned. "I didn't know anything about his little sister—the fact that she disappeared years ago."

Elly's eyes took in the folder I held. She raised one eyebrow, questioning.

"Yes, it's the file," I said. "Odell suggested I take a look at it." I think I snugged the file closer to my body as if to protect it.

"I'm glad he wanted you to read it." She spoke softly also, making our conversation relatively private. "I don't guess he talks about it much anymore. But I know it still bothers him and he wants to know what happened to her."

"You were here then?" Of course she was; she was born here.

Elly gave a short little laugh. "Oh, yes. I was around. I was the same age as Luanne. We were in the same grade. She was very, very smart. And friendly." Then a more serious expression came to her face, and she said, "When it happened, when she disappeared, all of our parents kept us close to home. We were all afraid, at least our parents were. Nothing like that had ever happened here. Mother would hardly let me out of the house." She leaned both elbows on the counter, her face close to mine. "It started raining that night and rained for about four days. Mother talked about how horrible it was, that little girl out there somewhere in that weather."

Elly looked up as one of the town lawyers came in. She

started to move to him but Janet said, "Yes, sir?" and cast her eyes over toward us as she went to the counter to get records for the attorney.

Elly straightened, gave me a quick smile.

"I'd better let you get to work," I said.

Leaning in closer again, she said, "Maybe, with your *considerable* investigative talents, you may see something that everyone else has missed . . . all these years." Her expression was half-serious, half-mischievous.

"Yeah, right," I said.

"Really, you may. I hope so." Her expression was fully serious this time.

I touched her hand and turned to go. "I hope so too," I whispered.

Chapter Three

As I drove away from the small downtown along Sir Walter Raleigh Street, I knew I wanted to delve into this cold case, not only because it was a mystery begging to be solved—something I can't resist—but especially because I truly wanted to help Odell. But as for a "cold case," this was surely one. Twenty-two years cold.

At the red stoplight for a left turn from Highway 64 onto 64/264, I glanced at the file folder resting on the passenger seat and almost unconsciously reached over and touched it. I wanted to get to it.

The driver in the car behind me gave a polite tap on his horn; the stoplight had turned green. I made my turn, heading for the Washington Baum Bridge over Roanoke Sound. I passed the fur-like marshes of the wetlands just before Pirates Cove, where dozens of large fishing boats were docked. The bridge rises high above the sound and at its apex the fishing village of Wanchese is almost visible down to the right. A quick glance to the left gives a clear view toward Jockey's Ridge, the highest natural sand dune on the East Coast. Then you start down the incline of the bridge to Nags Head.

After a short distance, I swung to the left at Whalebone Junction onto Highway 58, the north-south road we all call the Bypass, even though it bypasses nothing. Both sides of

the five-lane road (the middle lane for left turns) is clustered
with businesses. I was headed north up to Kill Devil Hills
and my little blue house, nestled in a cul-de-sac to the west
of the Bypass.

Parking my Subaru Outback under the carport, I ascend-
ed the steps on the outside of the house, carrying the Luanne
Wright folder with me. As I entered through the kitchen, my
parakeet, Janey, began chirping a greeting. She was very
loud for such a small bird. I'd had her now for almost six
years, and although female parakeets are said not to mimic
words, she does speak two not very nice words clearly and
distinctly.

I placed Luanne's file on the dinette table I've fashioned
into my desk, complete with computer, printer, and a two-
drawer file cabinet that fits underneath the table.

Across the room, the red light on my answering machine
blinked rapidly, signaling a new message.

I glanced automatically at my watch. Eleven-twenty. On
my way to the answering machine I had to step over the neck
of my bass fiddle, which almost always reclines on its side in
the middle of the living room floor. I punched the play-mes-
sage button that indicated the message had been received just
five minutes earlier.

It was one of those calls I hate. A woman's recorded
voice said, "There's no problem with your credit card, but
we can offer . . ."

Click. That ended that.

I went back to the dinette table and stood there a moment looking down at the folder. Typed neatly on the ear of
the folder was "Luanne Wright" and the year the case was
first opened—twenty-two years ago. To myself, I said,
"Okay, dear Luanne Wright, let's see what's in this file."
Sighing, I sat in the chair, breathed in deeply, and opened the
file.

Janey chirped.

"Talk to you later," I said. She chirped again, not wanting to be ignored.

First I took out the several newspaper clippings in the folder and set them aside.

Then I started with the very first page. It recorded when the first call was received at the sheriff's office from Mrs. Wright, Odell's mother, that her daughter had not returned home. The time was noted at 7:58 p.m. By the next morning, following three more calls from Mrs. Wright, Luanne Wright was listed as a missing person.

Then an all-out search was initiated. As Mabel had mentioned, many citizens responded—white and black. A command center was established at the fire station. Sheriff Claxton himself was listed as the coordinator of the initial search.

I read the pages carefully, and made a few notes on a legal pad as I went along, things that I planned to ask Odell to elaborate on.

After the initial report from Sheriff Claxton, virtually all of the reports were signed by the then Chief Deputy Julian Dickens. In one of the margins, a penciled note beside his name said "Retired." I assumed this may have been written by Odell or someone else in the sheriff's department. If Dickens were still around, he would be someone I would want to talk with. I jotted his name on the legal pad. There were other names, apparent leaders in the search, that I would list later.

As might be expected, the first searches were around the Manteo waterfront where Luanne was remembered as last being seen, and a favorite place of hers. The route she would have taken to return home, only about a ten- or fifteen-minute walk from the docks, was searched by a dozen volunteers. Nothing.

Another report listed the names of several boaters whose crafts were docked at the time at the Manteo marina. Nothing here, either. One boater thought he remembered seeing Luanne there at the docks but didn't pay any attention to her after that initial sighting. No larger boats had been docked there, boats that might have headed out to sea. Deputy Dickens noted that rain and wind moved in that morning but the searches went on, just as Mabel had said.

In a list of the volunteers, penciled notations had been noted beside some of the names. Such items were listed as "moved" or "deceased" and many of these notations were initialed and dated by O. Wright. Some of the dates were recent—only two or three years ago, well after Odell had joined the force.

Janey was quiet. Midday naptime for her. I checked my watch. I'd been at it close to two hours. Way past lunchtime, and I was beginning to feel it. I got up, stretched, and stepped into the kitchen to make an unimaginative ham sandwich. One sweet gherkin pickle on the side. A glass of water. I ate standing up. Not exactly a gourmet meal.

Thinking about the case, I sensed the frustration that Odell must feel. No leads at all. A few people had been questioned, and were quickly dismissed as not being "someone of interest."

With a sigh, I sat back at the desk.

Next I wanted to read the newspaper clippings. I figured I might get more of a sense of the real drama than I was from the routine reports. I separated the newspaper articles by dates. I would start with the oldest, written by someone at the local *Coastland Times* right after the search began. On the same date, there was an article in *The Virginian-Pilot* out of Norfolk. At that time, the paper had a news bureau at the Outer Banks. Like so many newspapers facing tougher economic times, the staff had been reduced, and there was no longer a fully staffed bureau here.

The first articles revealed no new facts for me—just that a search for a missing Luanne Wright had been initiated.

Articles a couple of days later were more telling. These articles, really what we'd call feature stories, concentrated on the number of volunteers, despite the continuing rain and wind. There were quotes from some of the leaders in the crew of volunteers. Years ago, a fire marshal, investigating the suspicious fire of a large warehouse, told me he always paid attention to those who showed up at the scene, sometimes even offering to help. He said such a person might very well be the arsonist.

I made notes of the names of leaders in the search.

Good photographs accompanied the feature articles. There was one that depicted the command center at the fire station, where an unsmiling, attractive youngish woman was giving out coffee and cookies to the poncho-clad searchers. The cutline under the picture identified the woman as Estelle Byerly Sasser. The man receiving the coffee, with his face turned smiling at the camera, was Devon Sasser, listed as her husband. I had already jotted down his name, as well as the young man beside him: Harvey Mitchell. His name was familiar to me. A local banker, I believed. A couple of decades younger, but I still recognized him.

At the end of the table, stood Mrs. Eula Wright, the mother of missing Luanne Wright. Several other volunteers, white and black, were in the background, all with rain gear but not identified.

Along with that feature story from *The Virginian-Pilot* was another picture of five searchers combing the edge of the Croatan Sound at the north end of Roanoke Island. One of those was a young Odell Wright. He wore a short windbreaker and baseball cap, his wet shoulders hunched as he bent over inspecting the edge of the water that practically lapped at his feet.

Yes, Odell had been there from the beginning. And he was still searching. I looked up from the file and stared out the window that faces me. I thought about how much he wanted to find his sister.

I wanted to, also. To find out what happened to that little girl on that day in May so long ago.

Chapter Four

The next morning shortly after eleven, I prepared to drive back over to Manteo to meet Odell for lunch at Darrell's.

Before heading out, though, I checked on Janey; she sulked because there had not been much commotion and activity, which she relishes. So I turned the radio on, volume up. "Want some raucous beach music?" She bobbed her head in the little awkward dance she does.

I got to Darrell's a couple of minutes before noon. Darrell's restaurant is on Highway 64, the main road into Manteo, and has been around since 1960. It's a favorite of many of the locals.

Odell's Dare County Sheriff's Department cruiser was already parked in front of the building. I went in and indicated to the young woman who greeted me that I was heading to the back booth on the right. Odell, in uniform except for a tie, his shirt open at the throat, half rose as I approached the booth, a slight smile on his face, his right hand extended.

"Appreciate your taking the time to meet with me, Odell."

He nodded pleasantly but didn't say anything. Odell is tall and straight in posture. He wasn't slumped like he was when I saw him in the interrogation room going over that file. His skin is coffee-colored; his eyes are clear and stare right at you. His nose is thin and aquiline. Reminds me of pictures of old Roman coins.

He had a cup of black coffee in front of him. Two menus were on the table, along with flatware wrapped in paper napkins. The young waitress came up, wearing a green Darrell's T-shirt and knee-length shorts.

"Give us a minute," Odell said. Then to me, he said, "Coffee?"

The young woman smiled and said she'd bring the coffee and then be back in a few minutes. We glanced at the menus. When she brought my coffee, Odell looked questioningly at me.

"Yes," I said. "Chef salad, ranch on the side." Odell chose the luncheon special, roast pork, mashed potatoes and green beans.

I had put the file and my legal pad to the far right of the table so it would be out of the way but easy to get to.

Odell tilted his head toward the file. "Thanks for going over the file, Mr. Weaver. I sure appreciate it."

"Please, Odell, drop the 'mister' bit. Just Weav is plenty good enough for me."

He smiled. "Yes, sir . . . Weav." Great smile. Really classical features.

I took a sip of my coffee. He obviously wanted me to say something about the file. He toyed with his cup. "I made some notes, Odell, that I'll ask you about." I looked across at him. "I just wish there were some great revelation I could tell you about. There's not. You and others have done a good job and looked at everything, it appears."

There was the slightest movement of his head. Waiting.

"I'd like for you to go over the list of volunteers with me. There are several I would like to talk with. Especially the leaders in the search, the ones who were always there."

"Yes, sir," he said.

"I was looking at some of the pictures in the news clippings. That was quite a setup at the fire station. The woman who served coffee and cookies. She was there all the time, I suppose. Maybe talk with her, too."

"Estelle Byerly Sasser." He got a faraway look in his eyes. "She was very emotional every time I showed up. Emotional with my mother too. She would get real teary, you know, almost crying, and hugging my mother." A trace of a smile. "Hugged me a couple of times, too."

"She still around?" I said. "I'd like to talk to her. She was there seeing every volunteer every day."

Odell got a puzzled look on his face. "You don't know?" He tilted his head. A bit of a pause before he said, "She's the Bear Woman."

Now it was my turn to look surprised. "The Bear Woman? You mean that woman who lives out in the woods toward East Lake and befriends . . ."

"Yes, befriends the black bears. Been out there more than twenty years now."

Of course, I'd heard of her, but I didn't actually associate her with a real living person. I almost thought of her as a local myth.

Odell said, "She moved out to the trailer she and her husband had right after most folks had given up the search." He rubbed his teeth lightly across his lower lip. "In fact, she broke up with her husband about that time, too. Later, I realized her marriage must have been unraveling for a while, but she put all that aside and did everything she could to help."

The waitress brought our food. A mist of steam rose from Odell's plate. "Plate's hot," she said to Odell. To me she asked, "Would you like some crackers?"

"Please." As she left, I said more to myself, "That was quick." Almost immediately she was back with three cellophane packets of saltines.

We started into the food without speaking for a moment or two.

He took a bite of his roast pork. "She'd probably talk to you." He chewed and swallowed. "I can tell you how to get out to her place."

"Good," I said. He gave me some simple directions. Then I opened the file and turned to the list of volunteers. "Can you check the ones who were around a lot, and are still around? I'd like to talk to some of them." I gave a mirthless chuckle. ". . . and the Bear Woman."

He nodded, a tired half-smile appeared. "Yes sir. I'll tell you, though, Sheriff Claxton and the SBI Agent Jeffrey Sutton talked to them and just about everybody else under the sun."

"What about Deputy Julian Dickens? He retired now? Still around?"

"Yes, sir. He's still around. But he had a stroke a few years back and doesn't much leave his house, except to go fishing. He can still talk, sort of. But he might remember something. Tell you the truth, Weav, I kinda doubt it, though."

He slid the sheet over to the left of his plate. I started to hand him a pen, but he pulled one out from his shirt pocket. "Three or four of these have died. Some have moved away. The three leaders, I guess you'd call them, were Herschel Creef, Harvey Mitchell, and Devon Sasser, the Bear Woman's husband. Or husband at that time, anyway. Mr. Creef died about four years ago. Harvey Mitchell is vice president or something at one of the banks up Southern Shores."

Although I didn't know Mitchell personally, I knew him by sight and I knew the bank he was associated with.

Odell clicked off three or four other volunteers who were around and that I might want to talk to.

We were both silent for maybe a minute or so while he continued to go over the list of volunteers. Then Odell spoke up. "I know you're wondering if maybe one of these . . . these volunteers, or maybe some other local person might be involved. I've wondered about that too, of course, over the years. But there's never been another disappearance of a young girl here in the county, and if it was someone here, some sort of serial killer . . ." He swallowed and controlled his voice before he continued. ". . . if it was some sort of a serial killer here in the county, I'd think he would have struck again during all these years." He shook his head. "I have to agree with what a number of folks said. It was probably a stranger to the area, not one of the locals. A tourist."

Chapter Five

I stared hard at his face. "Okay, Odell," I said, "I'd really like for you to keep talking, to hear what you have to say. Really fill me in on anything and everything you can. I'd like your take on what you think, how the search went—or didn't go—and your own personal theories, if you can to share them."

"To start with, Weav, let me say that the search for Luanne was as thorough and ongoing as could ever be expected." He puffed out a little sigh. "Let's face it, we're talking about a little black girl here, but everyone—white community and all—everyone pitched in to search. Even in the rain. And it rained for three days. Not a hard rain, but steady and chilly, with a northeast front that came in. The day she disappeared, it was as pretty a day as you could have. Sunny and warm. Then the weather changed, like it can so fast here. But that didn't stop everyone from searching."

Then, Odell with a piece of the roast pork poised on the end of his fork, said, "Luanne was friendly and everyone liked her. She loved coming down to the waterfront. She was always humming a tune or whistling. She walked to the waterfront from school or from home a lot of days. She was there that day."

He put the bite of pork in his mouth, chewed, and then said, "She was smart, too, and a good student. In fact, she'd done a report on the Freedmen's Colony here on the island that her teacher got her to read aloud to her class and to another the class down the hall. She even got a little brass medallion for the report that some group here in town gave her. She wore it all the time. Used to polish it. She was real proud of it. Hung with a little leather strip." He gave a short chuckle. "Maybe the title was not original but she called her report 'The Other Lost Colony.' That seemed really right to me. I've still got a copy of her report that my mother saved."

I knew something about the history of the Freedmen's Colony, and vowed to learn more. During the Civil War, Union forces had captured Roanoke Island, and following the occupations of the island, a number of former slaves had quickly sought refuge there. The Colony grew, but was totally disbanded after the war.

He said, "My great-grandmother was one of the people who came here, and she stayed on after the Colony was abandoned."

"That's quite a legacy, Odell."

He smiled. "I'm proud of it," Moving the green beans around with the tines of his fork, he speared a few. Before putting the fork to his mouth, he said, "Of course, in the beginning the search for Luanne focused on the waterfront area where some people remembered seeing her that day. She liked to watch the boats coming and going. She never went aboard any of the boats. Naturally boat owners were questioned, along with a number of other people. The names and details are all in the case file." He shook his head. "No suspects."

I ate silently, hoping Odell would continue talking.

He did. "We also searched back along the way she would have gone if she was going home." He paused. "And I say 'we' because I was in the middle of all of that, the searching. So was my daddy in the beginning. Sheriff Claxton was real good to me and my family. He came to the house to visit us more than once during the early days and weeks she was missing."

We had almost finished eating. I said, "When we leave here, I really would like to go with you over the route Luanne would have taken to go home. If you have time."

"Yes, sir. I've got time. Won't take but a few minutes. You can ride with me and then I'll bring you back here to get your car."

The waitress came up and asked if everything was good. We smiled and gave our approval and she scurried back to other customers who were beginning to crowd into both sides of the restaurant. Three people took the booth just behind me.

Odell lowered his voice and leaned forward. "Yes, Sheriff Claxton was real kind and supportive. I know I worried the dickens out of him because I hung around the courthouse and kept asking questions and going on the searches. I stuck to 'em like a tick."

"I assume the water areas were near the top of the list," I said.

"Oh, yes, sir. Those are the first places we searched, of course. All up and down the waterfronts, along Croatan Sound, Roanoke. Even over to Mann's Harbor."

I looked up at his serious face, his set jaw. "Ocean?"

"Yes, but not as much. Someone would have had to take her out in a boat, out through Oregon Inlet. Then go out to sea. None of the boats that were docked in Manteo that day went out, not that far. Most of them weren't big enough anyway. And the sheriff checked everyone."

I said, "You surely had a lot of people helping."

"Oh, yes sir. We had about three dozen volunteers in the beginning. Of course as the days went by, there were fewer and fewer. Gotta be expected." He gave the slightest shake to his head and looked down at his plate. "People began to give up hope." His eyes came back to me, a determination steeled there. "I didn't give up hope. Neither did Sheriff Claxton. He stuck with me and I stuck with him."

We finished out meals in silence. The waitress came back. "You want any dessert? Homemade strawberry pie?"

"Sounds mighty good, Gladys, but not for me. Mr. Weaver?"

"No, thanks. I'm fine."

She looked questioningly at us, trying to determine where to put the check, I presumed. "I'll take the check when you get a chance," I said.

After she brought the check, I said to Odell, "I'll meet you outside at your cruiser." I picked up my yellow legal pad and he carefully closed the file folder and tucked it under one arm.

We drove slowly in his cruiser. I sat in the passenger seat. Starting at the Manteo Waterfront, we traversed toward the main road, Highway 64. We stopped about a block from the highway. Odell pointed to a vacant lot. "From the waterfront, she would have walked this way, then cross the road at the stoplight. The stoplight wasn't even there then."

I could picture her, a slim girl in a thin white dress, schoolbooks hugged to her chest as she looked both ways then crossed the street. Whistling like Odell and Mabel had both said she was wont to do.

"You know, Odell, I've been thinking of course, and I don't believe she could have been abducted at the waterfront. Too many people around. And she wouldn't have gotten in willingly to anyone's car."

"Oh, no, she wouldn't have," he said. "She had strict orders about that and she obeyed them, I'm sure. She did what Mama and Daddy told her."

He eased the cruiser to the stoplight and waited for it to turn green. We crossed the highway to the road straight ahead. "She would go up this road for a block, then turn right." We turned right, then left. "Our house was up here only three more long blocks."

There was a scrub field on the right with low vegetation. On the left were three houses that appeared to be fairly new.

He stopped the cruiser. Inclining his head toward the houses, he said, "None of those houses were there then. These two blocks were just a field with scrubby pine trees."

I looked at him, and he looked back at me. Both of us were thinking the same thing, I'm sure.

This was where it happened.

It would be the most logical place. Someone parked here, waiting for her to come by. And bam! He got her.

But we drove on up to the third block and stopped in front of the clapboard house that used to belong to the Wright family. The house was in need of a bit of handiwork. Weeds grew in the yard. A kid's wagon was pulled over on its side, along with a few other odds and ends. "This is where we lived, and where my mother died. Now I live two blocks over that way." He flicked his thumb to the right. "Just me and Juanita, my wife. My daddy lives with us now. He has his own bedroom and bath built on to the house. But most the day he sits in the living room watching TV with the volume turned down so low I know he can't hear it."

"Juanita? She works, doesn't she?"

"Yes, sir. She's a biologist and works at the Coastal Research Institute. There on the road to Wanchese."

"I know the place," I said. "Wonderful, beautiful facility. Really a jewel set back there where you can't even see it without going up that long driveway to the building. The marsh and water behind it. Great view."

Odell took one last look at the house where he had grown up, sighed, and said, "I guess I better get on back to the courthouse."

When we got back to Darrell's for me to pick up my car, we shook hands and he said, "I appreciate you taking a look at the file."

"I just wish I'd come up with something. But I do want to talk with some of those volunteers . . . and the Bear

Woman." I got out and looped around in front of the cruiser to my car.

Odell had his window down. He leaned out to speak. "Who knows?" he said. "Just maybe . . . after all these years . . ." He shrugged, and backed away and was gone.

Chapter Six

When Odell drove away and I got in my Outback, I sat there a minute or more without turning on the ignition. Another customer approached in his car, assuming apparently that I was getting ready to leave. So I started my engine and backed out carefully, and he pulled right into the space I vacated. Eyeing the traffic, I waited until two pickup trucks went by, one of them turning into McDonald's next door, and then I pulled out into the middle turning lane and waited until a car passed on my right. I moved over into the right lane and headed out of Manteo.

I realized I flexed my shoulders and arched my back against the seat. I felt like I'd be doing heavy lifting. Well, I had been concentrating with Odell and trying my best to come up with something that could be helpful. No dice. Mentally and perhaps emotionally I felt like one of the more telling Southern expressions was most apt: *I felt like a stepped-on frog.*

Concentration will do that to you.

I just wanted to go home, call Elly, and sit on my deck in the mid-afternoon sunshine. Drink a cup of coffee, and hell, maybe light one of the cigars I keep for such situations.

Some of the vague weariness I felt, had to come from wanting so deeply to be able to solve the case of Luanne Wright's abduction, or at least come up with a sliver of a thought that might help. The only thing I could come up with now, as the next step, was to talk with several of the volunteers—for what good that might do—and to visit the Bear Woman. For what good *that* might do.

Oh, and I wanted to talk with the retired SBI agent who helped with the investigation, if he didn't mind getting off the golf course in Florida to answer my vague questions about an unsolved case that was twenty-two years old. And I would try for an interview with former Chief Deputy Julian Dickens, if his health permitted it. While I was at it, I'd give a call to my friend and SBI Special Agent T. (for Thomas) Ballsford Twiddy, also known as Balls. He was a good guy to bounce ideas off of, and as a law enforcement agent, he might have some insights I wouldn't.

As my mind worked, I was hardly aware of driving up the Bypass to my turn-off street. I pulled in under the carport and trudged up the stairs to the kitchen door. As soon as I went in, Janey chirped a loud greeting. I spoke to her and put my hand inside the cage, touched her gently with one finger, which she nibbled at equally as gently.

Then I did fix that cup of coffee, fished out one of my mild Honduran cigars from the cedar box, and took them both out on the deck. I placed the coffee on the wrought iron table, then went inside and brought the landline phone out and flopped in one of the webbed chairs. Before calling Elly, I lit my cigar and took a sip of the coffee. The sky was clear, the weather warm, and the sun made its way across the southwestern sky, lighting up the top of the live oak on the right side of my lot.

I dialed Elly's number at work. She answered on the first ring. "You sound very professional," I said.

"How has it gone today?" she said, her voice lilting with a smile.

"Oh, fine, so far," I said. "I had lunch with Odell Wright, and we talked about the file." Maybe my voice sounded a little downbeat. "Wish I could come up with something to help him. But there's not much chance, I'm afraid."

She hesitated a moment. "You okay?"

"Sure," I said. Then, determined to sound a bit more cheerful, I added in an easy tone. "Everything's fine, Elly. Really. Tonight? I come over?"

"Yes, I'd like that very much. Mother told me to invite you for dinner." She gave a short chuckle. "Your favorite: pork chops, stewed apples, and something else. I've forgotten. Oh, and her homemade biscuits."

"How could I resist?" I got a suggestive lift to my voice. "As for tasty morsels, you're my favorite."

"This is a business line," she said with mock disapproval.

"Six-ish?"

"Yes. That's fine. And I want to hear more about the lunch conversation."

A little later, after I had finished my coffee and smoked as much of the cigar as I wanted, I gave Balls a call. It went straight to voicemail, so I left a message. I had no better luck reaching Dickens or the former SBI agent who'd worked the case. Harvey Mitchell was in a meeting, and when the perky woman who'd answered the phone offered to give him my name and number, I told her I'd just try again later.

Frustrated, I put the case on the back burner and called Jim Watson. He's the leader of a little jazz combo I played with. Just started playing again about a year ago, and at one time I'd thought I never would play with a band again. That was because of my wife, Keely. She was a hell of a vocalist. Great jazz singer. Until she began to sink deeper and deeper into depression. Impossible to reach her. In the Washington area, I'd played in several combos with her. Then when she killed herself, I had no desire to ever play again. But gradually, and with Jim's urging, I started giving it thought. Played one or two gigs and actually enjoyed it. I was surprised. Even the songs we did that Keely used to excel upon didn't invoke as much sadness as I thought they would.

When I got Watson on the phone, I could hear recorded music playing in the background. He turned the volume down. "Glad you called, Weav. Just wanted to remind you about next week—Wednesday afternoon. We're featured from three to five at Scarborough Faire up in Duck."

"Right there at the little gazebo affair next to Island Bookstore?"

"Yep."

"The four of us? You, me, and Paul on keyboard, Dane on drums?"

"Oh, gonna be five of us. Tom Stevens, trombone, is joining us."

"Great. He's good. That'll be a nice sound."

"Well, the real season starts semi-officially before long —Memorial Day weekend—so I expect we'll be playing lots of gigs. Probably more than you want to."

And he was probably right. But just the same I welcomed that we would have a short, two-hour session there at a pleasant venue. In fact, after ending our telephone conversation I was mentally and emotionally basking in the feeling of pleasantness, of life being normal and easy: things like a nice easy jazz session, and dinner tonight with Elly and Martin and Mrs. Pedersen.

Wanting that feeling to last, I decided I'd wait and talk to the Bear Woman tomorrow.

Chapter Seven

That evening as I drove west across the bridge over Roanoke Sound toward Manteo, the trees in the distance were silhouetted black against the lowering sun. Still, it was light enough that the large pleasure and fishing boats docked at Pirates Cove glistened white, with rare flashes of bright gold from brass fittings.

Traffic moved smoothly as I swung right to go through Manteo and out toward the airport and Elly's street off to the left. I made the left and then another left and pulled in near the large live oak tree at the edge of Elly's driveway. Martin and his next-door little friend, Lauren, spent many a day playing under the umbrella-like spreading limbs of the live oak. One of Martin's rather beat up toy trucks lay on its side in the sand near the trunk of the tree.

As I cut the engine on my car and opened the driver's door, Elly came out on her low front porch and raised one hand in greeting, a smile on her face. Martin appeared right behind her and clutched onto one of her legs. He appraised me somberly. Their house was one of the original Sears houses from the 1930s that had been added to and modernized over the years, but still retained much of that earlier decade's appearance. Comfortable and homey.

I gave Elly a chaste kiss on one cheek. "Hello, Martin," I said. His expression didn't change.

"Say hello to Mr. Weaver, Martin," Elly said.

He mumbled something and turned back toward the screened door. Inside I could smell the delightful odor of Mrs. Pedersen's cooking. The living room always looked inviting and lived in. As usual, there was a lamp on at the end of the sofa and a section of *The Virginian-Pilot* folded to reveal the crossword puzzle, a passion of Elly's. I nodded toward the crossword. "Get it done?"

She gave a short laugh. "Yes, finished most of it during breaks at work. Once again, I zipped through one part because I remembered Walt Disney's middle name. They've used it before. Elias."

"Elias?"

"Yes, that comes up every so often. I believe I mentioned that to you the first time we talked about my crosswords." She looked good. She'd changed from the outfit she had worn at work and into a roomy, older pair of shorts, sandals, and a loose-fitting cotton top with short sleeves. Despite the casualness of her attire, she still couldn't hide the delightful curves and trim hips that lay underneath—not from my imagination. Her hair was pinned up in a somewhat haphazard ponytail. She stood close enough that I could smell her, that fresh cotton and sunshine fragrance she always seemed to emit.

Mrs. Pedersen came into the living room from the kitchen, a short apron tied around her waist. "Good to see you, Harrison. Supper's just about ready."

She had picked up from Elly the use of my full first name. "Smells awfully good, Mrs. Pedersen. Already making my stomach growl in appreciation."

She smiled and hurried back into the kitchen.

Trying not to be too obvious about it, Martin picked up one of his coloring books as if studying it carefully. He angled it so I could see.

"Great job of coloring, Martin," I said.

He flipped to the blank back pages of his booklet and

showed me a drawing he had done of a sand dune and a choppy sea.

"Very good indeed, Martin."

He nodded proudly, solemnly, and put the booklet on the coffee table. It lay beside one of Elly's history books, the title of which indicated it had something to do with the Punic Wars. Always tomes of ancient history—and crossword puzzles. That was Elly.

Dinner, or supper as Mrs. Pedersen called it, was excellent, as I knew it would be. The pork chops were perfectly cooked, tender and moist, set off with the cinnamon-sprinkled stewed apples, creamy corn Mrs. Pedersen had prepared by cutting the kernels off the cob, plus her hot, homemade-from-scratch biscuits. There was even some local honey that, when swirled with a pat of butter, was a mouth-watering delight on the biscuits. They had spoiled me with a number of suppers there at their house.

We had just finished the meal when, trying to make it sound casual and waiting until Martin had left the dining room and gone to play on the floor of the living room with four toy automobiles and making those car sounds, I got to the subject I knew Elly wanted to hear about: my visit today with Odell Wright.

Mrs. Pedersen had started to gather empty plates but stopped in mid-motion for an instant when she heard me mention Odell and going over the file about Luanne's disappearance. She said, "Oh, I remember that so well. So tragic. We were all worried about her and about our own children. I remember I kept Ellen close at home."

"Yes, I remember," Elly said. Then she looked at me. "So how did it go with Odell? Were you able to come up with something?"

"The conversation went well, of course. I like Odell. But as far as my offering any great insight—or breakthrough— the short answer is no. Absolutely not." I looked closely at her. "Maybe some of my ego got in the way thinking that maybe, just maybe, I might come up with something. But it is really, really, a cold case, and topnotch investigators went over everything, and then Odell has gone back over the file countless times."

Elly studied the tablecloth, tracing one fingernail lightly across the fabric, thinking. "At the very least, perhaps you can help him with closure on the tragedy."

"Maybe," I said. But I doubted it, actually. I didn't think he'd ever put it out of his mind until—and if—he found out what happened to her.

"You going to do anything further on it?" she asked.

"A little bit," I said. "I'm going to chat with a few of the leading volunteers, those still around." Then I grinned. "And I'm going to go out and talk to the Bear Woman. She was there at the headquarters the whole time, giving out coffee, cookies and things."

At the mention of the Bear Woman, Elly cocked her head and raised her eyebrows. "You sure? The Bear Woman?"

Mrs. Pedersen stepped back into the dining room. "What a strange situation with that woman, Estelle Byerly." Mrs. Pedersen said. "She was such a pretty young thing when that happened. She was married at the time, too. To Devon Sasser. I think they separated right about that time." She brushed a few crumbs into her palm at the edge of the table. She gave a slight shake to her head. "And then she became just a real recluse, living out there in their trailer with the bears."

"Odell said she'd talk to me," I said. "He gave me directions to get to her place."

"Do you really think she might be able to help?" Elly asked, her eyebrows still slightly raised.

"I doubt it," I said. "No more than anyone else. But she was there from the beginning of the search and stayed with it." I gave a tiny chuckle. "Tell you the truth, Elly, I'll admit I'm curious to see what she might be like."

Elly gave that mock look of disapproval she reserves for

me. "Always the reporter, aren't you? Just got to poke your nose into things."

By eight o'clock, Elly wanted to start getting Martin ready for bed. That was a signal for me to once again thank Mrs. Pedersen for the meal and to say my goodnights. Elly did step out on the porch with me and I kissed her and held her tight for several seconds. "Let's have a real date this weekend," I said.

She held herself against me for a moment. "I'd like that."

Driving back toward the beach and my house in Kill Devil Hills, I thought about how my wish for a pleasant and normal period, one without crises, appeared to be granted. At least for now.

Chapter Eight

The next morning, too early to start making phone calls, I started the day by playing a series of major scales on the bass using the bow. Worked steadily to get the proper intonation on the higher notes. Janey loves the extra noise and chirps along, totally off key. After a while I stopped, shook my head at the mess she always made as she managed to toss seed hulls around the outside of her cage. So I got the hand vacuum and cleaned up around her cage and then decided I might as well carry the trash out to the bin.

I was downstairs at the trashcan when I heard my phone ringing. By the time I got back upstairs, voice mail had kicked in. I crossed the living room, stepping over the neck of the bass, and punched in the play button.

It was Balls: "Okay, Weav, pick up if you're there. I'm only about ten minutes from your place. I'm in Nags Head. Heading up to Duck. If you're around I'll take you with me if you buy me lunch."

A typical Balls message: sort of a smart-ass tone to it. He's been a friend of mine since back in my newspaper days. I once was fortunate enough as an investigative reporter to uncover something that helped him solve a really knotty case. Since that time, he's called me his "Lucky Charm" and has let me hang around with him more than most investigators would. It also helps that I know when to keep my mouth shut; he knows I won't write anything that might compromise the investigation.

I punched in his cell phone number on speed dial. He answered at the first ring. A gruff, "Yeah?"

"Swing by," I said. "Like to go with you."

"Buy me lunch? That's the requirement."

"Sure." Then, "What are you doing down here? Why you going up to Duck?"

"None of your damn business."

"See you in a minute."

"Five."

"Okay."

Actually, it was less than five minutes before I heard the deep throaty rumble of Balls' classic old Thunderbird, his pride and joy, pulling into my cul-de-sac. As always, he backed into the driveway so he could make a speedy departure if he needed to.

Janey bobbed her head at me and chirped loudly as I hurried to the kitchen door. "Check with you later, Janey," I called. As I left I heard her say "Shit" as plain as could be.

I squeezed into the passenger seat of the Thunderbird. A tight fit because of a jumble of radio equipment and an on-board computer.

Balls grinned a greeting. He's a big man, and ruggedly handsome with his Tom Selleck-like mustache. Now a bit thicker in the middle, he still looks like if you tried to punch him in the gut it'd be like hitting a hard, wet bag of sand. Only thing that would be hurt would be your knuckles.

"You must have got an early start if you left Elizabeth City this morning and have already been in Nags Head," I said.

He drove out of the cul-de-sac. "I'm a working man," he said. "I don't sit around all day pecking away on a typewriter."

"Computer keyboard," I said.

"Whatever."

"Still miss a typewriter, though. Started my newspaper days with a typewriter."

He maneuvered onto the Bypass and pushed his speed up a bit above the 50-mph limit.

"You going to tell me why we're going to Duck?"

"Told you, none of your business."

I gave a little toss of my head. He'd tell me later. Maybe.

"Except that you're going to buy me lunch," he added.

We drove in silence until he got to the stoplight at Eckner Street. I glanced down to the east. It's the only place along this stretch of the Bypass where you can grab a glance of the ocean and I always check it out.

"Got your message last night," he said. What did you need?"

"The Luanne Wright file." I still wanted to get his take on it. "With Odell's permission, I went over the file about his sister. Actually, I didn't know anything about it until I saw him studying the report." I glanced over at Balls. "I guess you knew about it."

"Of course. But that was before my time. I had just started in Raleigh."

"Have you ever, you know, checked out that file?"

"Yeah."

I waited for him to say something else. We were at the intersection of the Bypass and Highway 12. He turned to the right and eased onto the two-lane Highway 12 to Duck.

He puffed out a sigh. "Poor Odell. He's never really gotten over it. Not much in that file that's helpful. Lot about the search itself. Several newspaper clips. Notes about where was searched. Mostly around the water, who some of the people were that were interrogated. Boaters who were docked there at the waterfront where she was last seen."

"Tourist, maybe?"

He shrugged. Both hands on the steering wheel. "A few locals were questioned, too. No leads." An SUV was ahead of us, sticking close to the 45-mph posted limit. Balls stayed a good distance behind the other vehicle. With a tilt of his head toward me, Balls said, "I know you're good and all that crap, but don't raise Odell's hopes . . . because I don't think you're gonna find anything in that file that will be helpful."

"Yes, I know," I said. Then I told him about my plans to talk with some of the leaders in the search.

He gave one of his dismissive "humpf" sounds.

I didn't have the nerve to tell him I also wanted to talk with the Bear Woman. He would really think that was far out, and perhaps I did too. My overriding curiosity was what was prompting that, I admitted to myself.

He slowed while the driver of the SUV apparently checked out an address. We approached Hillcrest Drive and after that the speed limit dropped down to 35. "But hell, who knows? You might see something that no one else has seen."

As we came into the city limits of Duck, the speed limit dropped again, now down to 25. It was difficult to hold it at that. But even this early in the season, there were families and couples strolling along the sidewalks, bicycles too, and there were several pedestrian crosswalks that you had to be fully aware of. We passed Scarborough Faire shopping center and then a short distance later at the Duck water tower, Balls turned into the parking area and found a spot in front of Duck's Cottage and Books.

Balls glanced at his wristwatch. "Coffee first," he said. "Then you buy me lunch." He cut the ignition, and looked over his shoulder. "You go get you some coffee and wait for me on the porch."

I nodded and got out of the car.

Inside, I was greeted with a big smile from Jamie, the owner, and I chatted with her a moment or two. We talked about a book we had both recently read about Hemingway's making of *The Sun Also Rises*. Other customers came up. I ordered a coffee and took it out on the porch and sat on one of the wooden chairs in the warm sun. I took a sip of my coffee. It was good. Nice and strong.

Looking across the parking area, I saw Balls standing in front of a store window, appearing to study the merchandise displayed. A man who looked to be in his late twenties, short beard, and rather baggy knee-length shorts, long-sleeve knit shirt, approached the same store front. He stood two or three feet from Balls and also seemed to be inspecting the window display.

They exchanged a few words as if discussing the merchandise. Then the man turned, nodded briefly without smiling and drifted away. Balls stood there a maybe half a minute longer before leaving the storefront and crossing back toward Duck's Cottage.

He lumbered up on the porch.

Chapter Nine

So that was why we'd come to Duck: for Balls to exchange a few words with that young man. He had to be one of Balls' confidential informants, or maybe another agent, maybe DEA or Homeland Security. I had no way of knowing.

"I saw you talking with that guy," I said.

"You didn't see a damn thing," Balls said. "Where's my coffee?"

"How do you want it?"

"Lots of cream and sugar," he said. He sat down in the chair beside mine.

I grinned, shook my head, and carefully set my coffee down and went back inside. I ordered another coffee from one of the young women working for Jamie. Jamie, tucked away at one end of the counter, was busy looking over some papers. I went back out with the doctored coffee. Balls stared off across the parking lot deep in thought.

"Thanks," he said, but without really looking at me.

"Something's up, huh?"

"None of your business," he said again, not with any emotion, though, just a flat statement as if thinking of something else.

It was obvious, however, that something indeed was up, something was brewing, something that worried Balls.

"Where for lunch?" I said.

"Huh?"

"Lunch. You said I had to buy you lunch."

"Yeah." He looked around, coming back to the here and now. "Oh, Coastal Cravings," he said. "That's always good." We finished our coffees and I put the Styrofoam cups in a recycle bin. Balls eased up out of his chair and I followed him. We drove south the short distance to Coastal Cravings, parked. Inside it was a little crowded, but not bad, and we got a booth right away.

A young woman in a large T-shirt and knee-length shorts brought us menus and filled the water glasses. Balls studied his menu in silence. I spotted fish tacos right away.

Balls looked up. "Ready?"

"Yes. You?"

He nodded and I signaled the young woman with a tilt of my head and a smile. I ordered fish tacos. She said they contained mahi-mahi. "Fine," I said.

Balls pointed at the lobster ravioli. "Oh, yeah," he added, "and bring a half pound of the steamed shrimp." For the first time since before Duck's Cottage, he grinned. "He's paying."

The young woman smiled. She didn't write down the orders. She was pretty and had great teeth, freckles across the bridge of her nose.

Glum again, Balls studied his water glass. He twirled it slightly back and forth with the tips of his fingers.

"You going to tell me what's up, or have I just got to read about it in the newspapers?"

He looked at me a moment, deciding what he could say. Then, "Don't much like it, but something is scheduled for tonight." He took a sip of his water. "Best you don't know."

I rarely saw Balls quite this solemn. It concerned me. "You okay?"

"Sure."

Then his cell phone chirped. He glanced at it, said, "Yeah?" and stood up to head outside to talk privately. He wasn't gone but two or three minutes and came back just as our server brought the steamed shrimp and an extra empty plate for the shells. Balls went right to the shrimp. He was fast. I took one, too. Figured I'd better. With Balls, you snooze, you lose. We were finishing the shrimp when our main orders arrived. They looked good.

With a wad of ravioli in his mouth, Balls said, "I'm gonna run you home . . ." He swallowed, ". . . after we finish, and leave my car at your place." He took another quick bite. "Somebody'll pick me up."

I studied him, eating slowly. The tacos were excellent.

The young woman refilled our water glasses and asked if we were enjoying our food. She wanted to know if we wanted anything else.

I looked at Balls. "Dessert?"

He shook his head, and she started to leave. But then he raised a hand; she stopped, smiling expectantly. "Ice cream. You have strawberry?"

"Yes, we do. One scoop or two."

"Two, by all means. Big ones."

She looked at me. "No thanks," I said.

"He's paying," Balls said.

After he finished his ice cream and I'd paid the bill, he said, "It'll be late when I come back for my car." The old grin came back. "So don't wait up for me. Go see your sweetie instead."

When we went out to the parking lot, I got in the passenger side and Balls stepped away a few feet and used his cell phone. It was a short conversation and he slipped the phone back onto his belt. We drove in silence, and when we turned into my cul-de-sac there was a dusty off-road Jeep parked near my house. I couldn't see the driver that well, but from what I could see it looked like the same man I'd seen Balls talking to up near Duck's Cottage. Balls backed his Thunderbird partly into my carport, but leaving room for me to get my Subaru out if I needed to.

As we got out, he retrieved a rumpled windbreaker from behind his seat. He didn't put it on but carried it in one hand. "Going with this fellow," he said.

I nodded. "Figured you were," I said.

He raised his free hand. "Don't wait up."

"Be careful," I said.

"Sure . . . oh, and thanks for lunch." He got in the passenger side of the waiting Jeep and they took off.

I watched them leave and then went up the stairs. Janey chirped happily when I came in the kitchen door. I spoke to her but didn't pause on my way through the sliding glass door in the living room and out to the deck, where I stood looking out. The afternoon sun had moved over to the west and south. Its rays touched the pine needles at the top of the tree on my left and made them look more golden than green. The Atlantic was over there to the east about a quarter of a mile away and I took a deep breath and imagined I could sense the faintly female scent of the ocean. It was a comforting place to be.

But I looked down at Balls' car and wondered what was up. I knew it had to be some type of operation involving other agencies, and I knew Balls well enough to sense that he was not satisfied with the way it was organized.

I went back inside, sat in the little chair by the phone, and called Elly at work.

"I've been wondering what you were up to, Harrison," she said. I love to hear her voice. There's still a trace of the "hoigh toide" accent that is fast disappearing on the Outer Banks.

"I've been with Agent Twiddy," I said.

"Uh-oh. You involved in something?"

"No, but I think he is." I started to tell her he'd left his car here but decided not to. "I don't know what, though. He wouldn't tell me."

"That's good," she said. Elly has come around to accepting that I'm a crime writer and as a result manage from time to time to get more than a little involved in investigations. But she does worry. I know that.

Trying to sound cheery and lighthearted, I said, "I thought I'd give you a break tonight and stay home."

"You sure you're not involved in . . . in whatever Agent Twiddy's involved in?"

I chuckled. "Promise."

To someone else she said, "I'll be right there." Then, to me she whispered, "Miss you."

"Same," I said.

I looked back at the late afternoon sun. My trip to Duck with Balls had taken all day, and now it was too late to go see the Bear Woman. Tomorrow. Tomorrow for sure.

Going back inside, I forced myself to practice the bass. After tuning, I played a series of major scales without vibrato. But I couldn't get with it. Janey chirped at the sound of my playing. She couldn't tell when I was a little off-key in the higher register, but I could, and I adjusted and mumbled something under my breath. Janey picked up on it and said, "Bitch."

"Okay," I said, "you've run through your complete vocabulary already today." She had started mimicking those words as I'd spent many hours with an exercise based on Mozart's "Requiem" that required a lot of crossing the bow back and forth over the strings. I was convinced that Mozart secretly hated bass players.

After a while I laid the bass back down on the floor.

That night I ate a light dinner of my own version of a chef salad, which I've proudly called World Famous, along with my World Famous dressing. The dressing is actually a modified Thousand Island or Russian dressing (mayonnaise and ketchup), but with a splash of sweet pickle juice and a few teaspoons of water, a pinch of sugar. I add julienned ham and three types of cheese to the lettuce.

Once or twice that evening I went out on the deck to glance down at Balls' car. I couldn't help but wonder what was going on and if it was dangerous. Well, more dangerous than usual.

I went to bed early and got up once during the wee hours of the morning and checked out on the deck again. The Thunderbird was still there.

At six-thirty the next morning I got up, took a quick shower, dressed in khakis and golf shirt, boat shoes, and slid back the glass door. The sun was up over the ocean and bright against my eyes.

The Thunderbird was still there.

Then the phone rang.

Chapter Ten

Hurriedly I stepped back inside from the deck and grabbed the phone and barked a hello, my voice urgent.

"Mr. Weaver? This is Deputy Odell Wright. I hate to call you this early but I'm down at the Outer Banks Hospital and Agent Twiddy wanted me to call you and ask you come down and pick him up."

"Hospital? Is Balls all right?"

"Yes, he's fine. Well, except for a slight laceration on his forehead."

"What happened?"

"There was a . . . an incident, Mr. Weaver. Last night up above Corolla."

"Drop the Mister, Odell. It's Weav."

"Yes, sir. But Balls—Agent Twiddy—is okay. Just about. He was here with one of the agents."

"I'll drive right down."

"I volunteered to take Agent Twiddy, but he said to get you."

"That's fine. I'll be there."

"Yes, sir. He'll be in the lobby or just outside."

"Odell?"

"Yes, sir?"

"The other agent? He . . . he okay?"

"Bullet wound to his left side. But he's going to be

okay, doctors say. Bullet went right through and didn't hit anything major. They didn't transfer him to Norfolk."

We ended the conversation and I uncovered Janey's cage and hurried downstairs. Backed carefully around Balls' car and headed out of the cul-de-sac and onto the Bypass. Traffic was light and I pushed my speed above the 50 mph posted limit. It was ten miles down to the Outer Banks Hospital. After the red-light signal at First Street, I hit all of the lights on green, making good time.

I pulled in under the portico in front of the hospital. Balls stood outside. He had a three-inch bandage on his forehead between his hairline and left eyebrow. Wearing that wrinkled windbreaker, he came to the passenger side. I had reached across to open the door but he beat me to it. He didn't smile, just sort of shook his head. He got in, slammed the door, and buckled his seat belt.

I studied his face. His hair wasn't combed and he needed a shave. "You look like shit," I said.

"Let's go," he said.

We drove out of the driveway to the stoplight at the Bypass. Waiting for the green light, I glanced again at Balls. "Okay, *now* you going to tell me?"

He was quiet and I didn't know whether he was going to answer me. The light changed and I turned left and headed back north. Then he said, "A drug bust. I didn't like the way it was organized. I wasn't comfortable with it soon's I got the details. And I was right." He huffed out a sigh, a tired sound. "Our folks expected one off-road vehicle coming down along the beach from Virginia. But there were two cars coming at us. We had enough people but that much company surprised us." He shook his head. "The bad guys thought they'd try shooting . They quit that after we returned fire."

He shook his head again. "But they hit Jeff Byrnes, the DEA guy you saw yesterday and the one who picked me up at your place."

"Hurt bad?" I asked.

"It always hurts. But it went through his left side, just above his belt. Didn't do any real damage, luckily, and he's in the hospital. I was with him."

"What happened to your head?" I drove in the right-hand lane, keeping slightly below the speed limit as I listened to Balls.

He touched the bandage with the tips of his fingers. "One young fellow didn't want to be arrested. Swung at me with the butt of a handgun. Didn't even need stitches. Just a butterfly bandage and a lump on my head. Just adds to my overall charm and good looks." Balls got his old shit-eating grin back for a moment. "Young punk won't be using that arm a his for a while."

Now it was my turn to shake my head. "All of them arrested?"

"Oh, yeah, all four of them. Oldest one was about twenty-two. Amateurs. They're all in the Dare County lockup." He puffed out another sigh. "Not telling you anything you won't read about in the paper or on the Internet anyway."

"Their drugs?"

He made a dismissive turndown of his mouth. "They didn't have all that much stuff anyway. Four blocks of cocaine and a bunch of marijuana." He twisted his head as if trying to relax his neck muscles. "Hell, there were seven of us and four vehicles." He pushed his back against the seat, shook his head. "Our operation wasn't well organized. Only thing we would've had to do was run two vehicles in front of them—about two o'clock this morning—and then scoot the other two vehicles behind them, cut 'em off. Or better still, stage a relayed surveillance to see where they were headed. Somewhere on the mainland, I gathered from the one who resisted me a bit." He glanced over at me. "Don't say anything about it not being well organized. Or write anything either."

"I won't," I said, and he knew I'd keep my word. When he mentioned the mainland, I thought again about saying something about my planning to talk with the Bear Woman. But I didn't.

We rode in silence until we got to the area with all of the fast-food places, the place we call French Fry Alley. "Want something to eat?" I asked.

He shook his head. "Naw, just wanna go home."

"You can take a nap at my place if you want to."

"Thanks, naw. Be off for a couple of days . . . I hope." He gave a short, mirthless laugh. "Like to see Lorraine. I got a wife, you know. Like to see her from time to time."

When we got to my house, I asked Balls if he wanted to come in for a minute or so, go to the bathroom, get a bite to eat?

He declined with a shake of his head. "Thanks for picking me up."

I watched him leave, and then I trudged back up the stairs. Felt tired. Yet it was not quite nine o'clock in the morning. I sat on the sofa for a few minutes, then went in the kitchen and fixed a half a bagel and microwaved a precooked sausage patty. Some orange juice. Brewed a cup of coffee. The whole time I was thinking about Balls and the crew last night, and what the action must have been. And I thought about Deputy Odell Wright and calling him to confirm that I'd picked up Balls.

After I ate, I went to the telephone and retrieved the number Odell had used to call me. I punched in the number. Odell picked up on the beginning of the third ring.

"This is Weav, Odell. Wanted to let you know that I picked up Agent Twiddy . . . Balls."

"Yes, sir. Appreciate it. He wanted me to go home."

"Oh, I'm sorry. I guess you were with them last night. You're probably trying to get some sleep."

He gave a short laugh. "I can't really get to sleep. Too keyed up."

"Yes, and it doesn't help that I call you on the phone."

"That's okay," he said.

We signed off and I sat there a few moments, staring vacantly across the room. Janey cocked her head at me but didn't chirp. Then she turned her attention to what was left of the millet sprig. I rose and walked to her cage, put my hand inside, wrapped my fingers around her and brought her outside, cuddled against my cheek. She tolerated that and actually seemed to enjoy it. The male parakeets that I'd had wanted to pretend to fight, not cuddle. She was definitely female, and she was a comfort. I put her back in her cage and she bobbed her head and chirped. "You're okay, Janey," I said.

I went back to the phone to call Elly at work.

She answered, "Register of Deeds office, Elly Pedersen speaking."

"That sounds formal and businesslike," I said.

Her voice soft, she said, "I've been wondering where in the world you were."

"I had to go down to the hospital to pick up Balls—Agent Twiddy."

"I know that," she said, still speaking softly but with a touch of irritation in her tone.

"He's okay, but—"

"Mabel told me. I'm just glad you weren't involved."

"I told you I wasn't." Now there was a touch of irritation in my voice.

She sounded more relaxed, as she said, "I know you said you weren't but sometimes you get involved even when you don't intend to . . ."

That was the truth, and I knew it.

Chapter Eleven

An hour later, I parked in a bumpy small lot off Sir Walter Raleigh Street across from Downtown Books. The courthouse was only a couple of doors up from me. I stepped up on the porch at the front of the courthouse, built in 1904, a year after the Wright Brothers' flight, and went inside. Before going upstairs, I stuck my head into the Register of Deeds office to speak to Elly. She was in the back and I asked Janet to tell Elly I'd be upstairs on business.

In her teasing singsong voice, Janet said, "Be happy to tell her, Mr. Weaver."

With a grin I thanked her and went up to the sheriff's department, stepped into Mabel's office. She sat behind her desk, completing a phone call. As she hung up, she gave one of her warm smiles. "I understand from Odell you had quite a time reading through the file." She indicated the thick folder that was at one corner of her desk. I recognized it right away. The smile still there, she inclined her head toward the chair in front of her desk. "Sit down a minute."

She nodded at the file. "It's grown quite a bit over the years. But I'm not sure how much in there was really useful. Mostly it talked about, well, dead-ends, about things that didn't work out. Places that were checked, people who thought they knew something . . . but didn't."

I cleared my throat. "Actually, what I wanted to talk

with you about, Mabel, is your impression of some of the people who did the main searching. I plan to talk with several of them."

She said almost the same thing Balls had said: "Well, good luck on that."

"Odell indicated to me the ones who are still around. I thought I'd start with them." A slight shrug. "I know. It's not likely to lead anywhere but I want to do what I can to look into this . . . this case."

"I understand," she said, eyeing me closely.

"At the same time, I don't want to in any way give Odell a sense of false hope."

"I agree," she said. "He's suffered enough. It killed his mother, I'm sure, and has just numbed his father so that he's not . . . not even really aware anymore."

I pretended to look at my notes. "Thought I'd start with a couple of the leaders in the search—Harvey Mitchell and Devon Sasser. Also, retired Chief Deputy Julian Dickens."

"Julian is out fishing just about every day. No trouble finding him. As for Devon Sasser, I know he travels in his job, and . . ." She paused a moment and I watched her face. ". . . and Harvey Mitchell is now a big shot with one of the banks."

"Harvey Mitchell?" I said, one eyebrow raised. "I sense that he may not be one of your favorites?"

Mabel was a tad reluctant but after a breath she did say, "No, he's not." A trace of a smile. "No love lost either between Devon Sasser and Mitchell."

I waited, watching her expectantly.

"It was a long time ago, and I'm not saying anything that's not common knowledge." She took in a breath. "Harvey Mitchell was having an affair with Estelle Byerly Sasser, Devon's wife. That was just about the time Devon and Estelle broke up, and she went to live out on the land she had on the mainland near East Lake." Mabel stared at me. "That was not the first time—or the last—that Harvey Mitchell had an affair. I'm not spreading rumors when that's pretty well known."

"Was it the affair or the breakup of her marriage that made Estelle move out to the mainland?"

"No one knows for sure, of course. Devon Sasser has never been much to write home about."

"Is that when Estelle became the legend, the Bear Woman?"

"It was some time after that, I guess. She became a real recluse. A hermit, really. And people over the years have called her the Bear Woman. Lots of folks, I suppose, don't even know her real name."

I took a deep breath and plunged right in. "Well, I wanted to talk with her, too."

A very puzzled look from Mabel. "She wasn't in on the search."

"No, but she was there at headquarters every day giving out coffee and donuts and things. She saw and talked with all of the volunteers." I started to mention how concerned she'd seemed for Odell and his mother but I decided to hold off on that.

Mabel cocked her head at me. "You sure it's just not, you know, curiosity on your part?"

I smiled in return. "Well, yes, you know it is partly, but just the same, from what I've read in the file and talking with Odell, no one ever really questioned her about what she thought. So, yes, a lot of curiosity, if I'm honest, but also she just might have some ideas that no one else has ever expressed."

Mabel had to agree, maybe a bit reluctantly, but agree nonetheless.

Leaving Mabel's office, with sincere thanks for being forthcoming with me about some of the town relationships, I went to look for Odell. I couldn't find him in any of the offices, but as I looked out one of the windows I saw him parking his cruiser on Budleigh Street and getting out, coming to the side door. I scurried down the stairs and met him just as he prepared to open the door. We stood on the sidewalk.

Leaning forward so I would not have to talk loudly, I said, "I plan to go on out and try to talk with Estelle Byerly Sasser."

"Now?"

"Yes."

"The Bear Woman. She may talk to you. She may not."

"I know," I said.

"Want those directions again?"

"I think I remember."

"That rutty little road less than a half a mile or so beyond Stan's Market."

I nodded.

"Good luck," he said. Then he turned to go in the building. With his hand on the door, he gave the slightest of shrugs. "Who knows? Just maybe . . ."

And he went inside and I walked around the front of the courthouse to Sir Walter Raleigh Street to get my car and head out toward the Bear Woman's place.

Chapter Twelve

It was not quite eleven o'clock as I pulled onto Highway 64 and headed west toward the older Mann's Harbor Bridge. I liked going across the Croatan Sound from the northwest end of Roanoke Island. Sun sparkled on the water of the sound and the water looked peaceful and mostly flat except for the little pinpoints of sun.

I made my turns into Mann's Harbor and in a little ways passed Stan's Market on the left. A half a mile or so up the highway I still didn't see the tiny road Odell told me about. Close to a mile later I spotted it just as I passed it. I had to go up a bit farther until I found a place to turn around and come back.

The road was not much more than a rutted pathway. My Outback was high enough that if I stayed out of the deeper ruts, the undercarriage cleared okay. About fifty yards in, the road smoothed out considerably. Tacked to one of the trees was a faded hand-printed pasteboard sign that said "Beware of Bears." I planned to.

Along both sides of the road, pine trees grew close together. There were a few hardwood trees, including a large hickory that stood somewhat alone. Low brush came close to the road. But then, with the sun high overhead, the trees and undergrowth gave way to something of a pasture with low grass or weeds of some sort. It looked almost idyllic. Beyond the pasture another bank of trees stood like a fortress. I figured that was where the bears had to live.

The road bent around in a long curve to the edge of the clearing, and then through a low growth of trees I caught a glimpse of a green structure, a relatively small house trailer. I drove closer. The trailer sagged at one end; the paint was streaked with darker material from the surrounding scrubby pines. Patches of pine needles bunched on the roof. At one time the trailer had probably been painted a medium green. A power wash would help, if the pressure didn't knock the trailer down. There was a clearing off to one end of the trailer and a smooth pathway leading to the trailer's entrance.

At the clearing, a woman bent over slightly, working in what appeared to be a small garden, maybe vegetables.

As I stopped the car and cut the engine, the woman straightened up and eyed me. She didn't smile or frown, just studied me.

I tried to look friendly. "Mrs. Sasser?" I said.

She didn't appear she would respond. Then she said, "It's Byerly. Estelle Byerly."

"Yes, ma'am," I said. I told her my name and slowly approached her. She leaned one hand on a short-handled shovel. The blade of the shovel was worn to dull silver over the years. A worn hoe lay on the ground beside her. Sprouts of leeks or spring onions popped out of the ground, and there was the beginning of what looked like lettuce. At the far end of the garden, four small tomato plants clung to stakes. The tomato plants caught the morning sun.

Estelle Byerly wore what were probably tan slacks, rolled up at the ankles, exposing sockless ratty looking sneakers. A sweat-stained loose fitting shirt covered her upper body. She didn't wear a bra and didn't appear to need one. Her hair was uncombed and she used her free hand to push back some of it from her face. No makeup. Her eyes were very bright blue, with little crinkles at the corners. It was easy to see that at one time she had been a beautiful woman.

Her voice flat, expressionless, she cocked her head to one side and said, "You come to see the bears?"

"No," I answered a tad rapidly. "I'm a writer and I wanted to talk with you about something that happened a long time ago."

That deadpan look at me, waiting. She took a tentative step toward me, still holding the short shovel in one hand.

I tried a reassuring smile but didn't move. "As a writer, I'm looking into the disappearance twenty-two years ago of little Luanne Wright."

Her body stiffened. Her eyes glared at me, jaw set. She shook her head violently. "No, no," she said. "I don't talk about that."

For just a moment, I thought she might cry, but then a resolute firmness took over again. "You can leave now," she said. It was not a request; it was a command. She jabbed the shovel into the soft ground and put both hands on her hips. A formidable stance. "I don't want to talk to you and I don't want you on my property." The chin jutted forward. "Leave," she said.

I tried one more time. "But you were there at the beginning, helping with coffee and everything at the headquarters and I thought you might know something that would help in some . . ."

She cut me off. "Leave, I said."

"Okay, okay. I didn't mean to upset you, I just wanted to talk . . ."

She put a hand on the shovel's handle. She glared at me.

I shrugged and held my palms upturned. "All right," I mumbled, and stepped back to the door of my Subaru. "Sorry to bother you, upset you."

She didn't respond except with the set of her face and her eyes.

Then at the far edge of the clearing, I was sure I saw a large black bear—at least he looked large to me—watching me prepare to leave. I looked again but he had disappeared.

I got in my car, started the engine, backed around, held one hand up in a halfhearted wave and left her standing there watching me drive away. In the rearview mirror, I thought I saw her trembling, whether from anger or from sorrow, I couldn't tell.

Out on the highway, I drove rather slowly, thinking about Estelle Byerly and her reaction to my broaching the subject of Luanne Wright's disappearance. It was curious. And much more—what?—emotional, almost hostile, or maybe defensive than I expected; I wasn't sure.

As I passed Stan's Market I automatically checked my gas gauge. I didn't need any for a while. I crossed the bridge and drove straight to the Budleigh Street side of the courthouse. Balls' Thunderbird occupied one of the reserve spots. I drove around the block to the little parking area off Sir Walter Raleigh Street where I had parked earlier. As I got out of my car, I could smell the coffee from the shop upstairs. It smelled good, and I realized it was past lunchtime and I hadn't eaten. Oh, well, later.

Going around to the front door of the courthouse, I looked in the Register of Deeds office but Elly was busy talking with a paralegal from one of the attorney's office. She gave me the tiniest nod and smile. I went on upstairs.

Balls and Odell were in the windowless interrogation room, both leaning forward, elbows on the metal table, talking quietly. I tapped lightly at the doorframe. Balls glanced over his shoulder. Odell sat on the other side facing me.

Balls said, "You might as well come on in." The bandage on his forehead was about half the size it was when I picked him up at the hospital.

I took the chair beside him. "You're healing good," I said, motioning to the bandage.

"I'm tough," he said. Then he gave me that blank cop's stare. "Odell tells me you went out to bother that Bear Woman."

"Yes."

Still looking at me he said, "You see anyone else out there?"

"I think I saw a bear when I was leaving. But I didn't stay around. And, no, I didn't see anyone else."

They both were silent. I guess waiting for me to continue. "She wasn't real friendly," I said. "At least she wasn't friendly when I told her I wanted to talk about the search for Luanne."

Balls said, "What did you expect?"

"Well, I didn't expect her to tell me to leave, get off her property as soon as I mentioned that I wanted to talk with her about . . . about that."

Odell frowned. "That *is* curious." He took his elbows off the table, leaned back. "She was real emotional when Mother and I came around the fire station where she was, but she certainly wasn't, you know, hostile or anything."

"Maybe my bringing that period up reminded her of when her marriage went south. She made a point of saying her name was Byerly and not Sasser." I declined to say anything about the affair Mabel said Harvey Mitchell was having with Estelle.

Balls frowned. I wasn't sure he got the connection with Sasser. Then he said, "So, soon as you got there she wanted you to leave?"

"No, not at first. First she wanted to know if I wanted to see the bears. Then I told her why I was there, and that's when her whole attitude changed."

Balls again: "You didn't see anybody else?"

"No," I repeated. "What's all this about seeing somebody else?"

They were both silent for a long moment. Balls spoke: "That thing the other night. It appears those guys were headed there near East Lake, pretty close to where you were today, to meet some of their cohorts. Good ol' boys involved since the fishing is slow—and there're no wildfires for them to hire out to fight."

Odell got one of those slight wry smiles, listening to Balls.

"Need to have a little come-to-Jesus talk with those boys," Balls said. "They live near the Bear Woman. Just maybe she might be involved."

Odell gave an expression like he wasn't sure. "I don't know, Agent Twiddy, she and those neighbors of hers are pretty much enemies. She supposedly yells at them a lot and threaten them if they get close to her bears."

Balls shrugged. "We'll see." He turned that cop stare at me. "Meanwhile, you stay away from her. Okay?"

"She doesn't want me around anyway," I said. "I wasn't planning to go back."

But I did. Though not the way I planned.

Chapter Thirteen

What I intended to do the next couple of days was to talk with Harvey Mitchell and Devon Sasser, maybe some others. But I didn't have any luck with either of the two.

First I went to Mitchell's bank in Southern Shores. A very pleasant young woman there told me he would be visiting the bank's branches in Columbia, Rocky Mount and down in Lumberton for the next two days, and would I please come back. I told her I most definitely would. Although she looked at me expectantly, I didn't tell her what I wanted to talk with him about.

I rechecked Devon Sasser's residence in the phone book. Turned out he lived in Kill Devil Hills, only a half a mile or so from where I lived. I dialed his number and after three rings got an outgoing message saying he would be traveling on business for a "short period" and to please leave a message and he would return the call when he was available. I didn't leave a message.

Okay, striking out.

Somewhat depressing, and partly, I knew, because I was chasing after something that would probably lead nowhere at all.

So I decided to go fishing. Heck, I might even run into retired former Chief Deputy Julian Dickens, and I wanted to talk to him, too. Knowing how Mabel knows damn near everything in the county, I called her to ask again where Dickens usually went to fish.

"As pretty as it is today, he's probably already fishing down at the south end of Coquina Beach," she said. "It's a favorite place of his."

I decided to head out.

I had some bait shrimp in the freezer. Not as good as fresh; but I had frozen it in a Ziploc bag filled with water. That assured that when thawed it was almost like freshly caught shrimp. I put that in a little pan of water and went downstairs to the utility room and got my surfcasting rod, sand spike, a small container of extra bottom rigs, hooks and weights, plus the five-gallon white plastic bucket into which I piled the tackle. Upstairs I would dump a supply of ice in the bucket and insulate the ice with layers of newspaper. The shrimp would go in there, too, along with a handy fish knife.

Thirty minutes later I drove south toward Coquina Beach. When I parked at the far end, the sun was still fairly high behind me and it glistened and sparkled the water. The tide was still high, but receding. Fishing would have been better, I felt sure, to have started on the incoming high tide, but this was fine. The act of fishing was more important to me than actually concerning myself with whether I caught anything. I was out here; it was a beautiful spring afternoon, and to the north the only other persons in sight were a man and a young boy fishing a hundred yards from me, up near the pavilion and bathhouse.

Looking down to the south, I saw a lone fisherman. He was maybe a hundred and fifty yards away. That had to be retired Julian Dickens. I didn't want to bother him right away. Figured it best to busy myself fishing, leave him alone until he got used to seeing me up to the north of him.

On the third cast out, I was satisfied with the distance and placement. The weighted rig—I only use two ounces—and the two hooks of the rig were plumb with shrimp. I had kicked off my old sneakers and stood barefoot in the cold edge of the water. As a low wave came in, I backed up. My feet were getting used to the water and the wet sand. I kept the butt of the rod against my hipbone and supported the rod with my right hand, making sort of a triangle. One finger of my right hand held lightly onto the monofilament line.

I had just stepped back from an incoming foam of low surf when I felt a sharp tug on the line. I flicked the rod back, setting the hook, and began to reel in. A few yards out from the surf, the fish splashed up to the surface. Not a big one, but fun. When I brought him up to the sand, and secured the butt-end of the rod in the sand spike, I picked up the fish and began unhooking him. It was a croaker—and he made that croaking sound—as he squirmed in my hand. He was about thirteen or fourteen inches long but I didn't want him and I waded back to the ocean's edge and released him. He rolled over once in the surf and then swam swiftly away.

Checking down to the south, I saw Dickens watch me bring in a fish and release it. I kept a half-eye on him, biding my time before strolling down there to try to engage him in conversation.

I re-baited the hooks and cast out again. The one thing about fishing is that when you're doing it you don't think about much anything else, just the next possible strike, and the next fish. Such concentration usually works, too. And it did, mostly, this morning. However, I caught myself from time to time drifting back to the case of Luanne Wright, wondering. And I wanted to get down the beach and talk with Dickens.

I was absently reeling in, set to cast out again, and when I got close to the beginning of the rolling surf, not more than fifteen yards out, there was another sharp hit on the line. And I brought him in—a very nice size flounder, plenty big enough to keep and make a couple of fillets. Unusually large for this early in the season. I put him flopping in the bucket with the ice. This was about enough fishing for me, but I did cast out one more time. Ready to walk down to Dickens. But the young boy from up the beach had started walking toward me. I smiled at him.

He said, "Looks like you're having some luck. We're not doing much."

There was another strike on my line. "There's something of a hole out in front of me. I'm getting ready to quit . . ." I kept reeling in. "Why don't you two come on down here?"

I pulled in another croaker, even larger than the first one. "You want him?" I asked.

"Sure," the boy said. "I'll get my dad."

Using my feet and one hand, I scooped out a deep impression in the wet sand. "I'll put the fish here," I said. "I'm going down to speak to my friend . . ." I inclined my head. "Then I'm packing up and leaving."

Securing my rod in the sand spike, I walked—hopefully nonchalantly—toward Julian Dickens. He eyed me as I approached. I did a big smile.

"Looks like you're having some luck," he said, echoing the boy. He was a big man, probably seventy, long muscular suntanned arms and hands the size of hams. Except for a slight downturn on one side of his mouth, there was no evidence of the stroke he had suffered. In retirement, he hadn't bothered to shave for a couple of days. He wore a baseball cap, pulled tight against his mostly gray hair.

I introduced myself but we didn't shake hands because he still held his fancy surfcasting rod with both hands. But he didn't look unpleasant. There was almost a smile. "I know who you are," he said.

"And I know who you are," I said. "Mabel, at the sheriff's office, said I'd probably find you down here."

"Mabel knows everything." He looked at the ocean. He reeled in and cast overhand not far into the surf. "Trying for pompano," he said. Still pleasant.

"Bit early?"

"Yep, but who knows?" Now he held the rod with only one hand, his left arm down by his side. His eyes toward the surf, he said, "Why you looking for me?"

"Wanted to talk to you about a very old case you worked on."

"I don't remember any of the old cases I used to work on. I'm retired." But he grinned. Had a nice look to his face. Probably a more relaxed ex-lawman than he was when he was working.

"Got to talking with Odell Wright and went over that old file about his sister, Luanne, who disappeared twenty-two years ago."

He looked hard at me and shook his head. "Jeeze. Talk about cold cases. You really are trying to dig into the past."

"I know," I said. "And I don't really think I'll have any luck, but I thought I'd give it a shot. Like you say about the pompano, who knows?"

That grin again.

"I wanted to get your opinion. Your view of what might have happened."

"What happened was somebody snatched her and did away with her somewhere. We never found her body and we never had any real suspects. End of case." He tugged lightly on his line, but there was nothing there. He reeled in, checked his bait, and cast out again. For the pompano, he was using sand fleas for bait. Don't know where he got them this time of year.

Doggedly, I didn't want to let the subject go. "I thought I'd also check with some of the leaders in the search."

He gave me another sidelong smile. "I know what you're thinking. Always a good place to begin." He shook his head. "I did the same thing. Talked with all of 'em. Harvey Mitchell, Devon Sasser, Creef. He's dead now. Nothing."

"You think it was local? Or a tourist, visitor, someone passing through?"

"In the beginning I thought it might be local, and I looked real hard at a number of folks." He made a little face. "Nothing, and over the years, with nothing else like that here, I began to go along with the common belief that it was done by a stranger to the Outer Banks."

Something hit his line. He set the hook and reeled in. An ugly fish. What some of us call a blow fish, others a puffer because it does puff up, its spiny barbs sticking out looking vaguely menacing. With his hand wrapped with a short, stained cloth, he took the fish off and tossed it in a long underhanded loop back into the ocean. He re-baited. This time with a shrimp on one of the hooks.

I waited for him to cast out. "Reading the file, I can surely see it was investigated thoroughly." Now it was my time to shake my head. "I really don't know what in the hell I might find, and maybe it's just partly curiosity on my part, but I wanted to look into it . . . maybe just as sort of a favor to Odell. I like him."

There was almost an expression of sympathy on Dickens' face. "I know what you mean," he said softly. "Odell never got over it. Neither did his mother or daddy."

We talked a bit more and then I thanked him and wished him luck on the pompano. He shook my hand before I left him and he said he wished me luck, too, but that he didn't hold out much hope.

Neither did I. And when I walked back up the beach to retrieve my tackle and the bucket with the flounder, I moved slowly and wasn't feeling at all happy despite being at the ocean.

Leaving Coquina Beach, I drove north, though Nags Head and I continued past Kill Devil Hills and went on up to Kitty Hawk and Carawan's Seafood. Bob said he'd be happy to filet my founder, as long as I let everyone know I caught him on one of his shrimp. This was a banter we had shared before. I waited around while he went in the back and took care of the flounder. I picked up a fresh little jar of horseradish from the cooler and paid for everything when Bob brought my filets out.

I figured I'd cook a fish dinner for Elly, maybe even tomorrow night.

Thinking about that made me feel better.

Chapter Fourteen

When I got back to my house I called Elly and told her about the fishing (but not about chatting with Julian Dickens) and invited her to dinner the next night when I would cook the fillets.

Elly said, "I accept your kind invitation, sir, for dinner tomorrow night, but only on one condition."

"Yes?"

"That is if you will let me drive my car to your house. There's no sense in your making another roundtrip over here, pick me up, then have to bring me back."

We agreed that she would drive over, even though I protested mildly that it didn't seem the Southern gentlemanly thing to do.

While waiting for Elly the next evening, I had cleared the kitchenette table that I used for my desk overlooking the southern exposure. I could look out the windows and track the sun from the southeast in the morning until it disappeared beyond the pine trees to the west.

I made a salad and vinaigrette dressing and put them in the refrigerator; prepared two potatoes for baking by rubbing the skins with olive oil and wrapping them in paper towels; and I had marinated the fillets in milk several minutes before shaking them in a mixture of salt, pepper, and cornmeal in a large Ziploc bag. Putting a skillet on the stove, and the potatoes in the microwave, I was ready to start pushing buttons when Elly arrived.

A few minutes before six, I saw her white Pontiac pull into the cul-de-sac. I stepped out on the deck. The sun had begun touching the pine trees to the west. The air was warm and the sky clear and still blue. I waved a greeting and went down the outside steps to meet her as she came up.

Elly wore a pinkish cotton blouse, her white cardigan sweater, and an off-white plain skirt and sandals. She had her dark brown hair pinned back; not a ponytail but getting close. I gave her a hug and light kiss on the lips. She smelled good, as always. I didn't want to let her go. But it was rather awkward standing on the steps, plus she carried a plastic-wrap-covered plate. She had to maneuver the plate away from between us to keep me from dislodging it.

"Mother sent you some fudge brownies she baked this afternoon," she said, skillfully extricating herself from my embrace and handing me the plate.

"Wonderful," and they were too, moist and chocolaty, as I knew they would be, because I pinched off a corner and ate it while Elly settled in the house.

She helped me with the final preparations, getting iced tea for both of us. I offered her a glass of wine, but she declined and said the tea would be fine. I kept a little wine for guests. A few years earlier, after Keely died and I went on a walking-around bender that lasted for months, I quit drinking alcohol. Actually became afraid of it. The fear had lessened but that hadn't changed my decision.

Busying myself in the kitchen, I got dinner ready in record time while Elly got the salads out, dressed, and ready to eat. The flounder fillets turned out well. Crispy and a little flaky but the consistency was good, firm enough for good-size bites. I prefer potatoes baked in the oven, but the microwave does the job and split open with butter and sour cream, plus a sprinkling of grated cheese and bacon bits, they were delicious. A little basket of crusty Italian bread I'd picked up at Harris Teeter and we were in business.

When we finished eating, I made each of us a cup of espresso. "Ah, shades of Paris," Elly said, where we'd finished each meal with an espresso.

"I know Balls and Lorraine will be happy to go back," I said. "She'll even volunteer to be our chaperone again."

"Um-huh," Elly said with a smile.

We had moved to the sofa with our espressos, setting the cups and saucers on the appropriately named coffee table. Elly tilted her head and smiled wickedly at me. "I'm not at all sure who believed that chaperone business before, and I know no one would buy it a second time."

As we finished the coffee, she said, "Shall we do the dishes?"

"They can wait," I said. I put my arm around her and pulled her to me. "*I* can't wait, though. Not being this close to you and having you all alone."

"I know," she breathed, and we kissed, long and hard. When we ended the kiss, she said, "Oh, my."

I stood and pulled her up against me and we pressed hard against each other and kissed again, and after the kiss she said again, "Oh, my . . ."

We hardly made it to the bedroom, shedding clothes as we went. I wanted to look at her a moment or two before even touching her. "No wonder artists paint women," I whispered, and began to plant kisses on her as she lay on the bed.

Afterward, she smiled a little sleepily, and said, "Back to Paris sounds like a wonderful idea . . . and being here like this reminds me of being there." She raised herself on one elbow and glanced at the clock beside the bed.

"I know, I know," I said.

"Yes, I'd like to see Martin before he goes to bed. Mother will probably let him stay up a little bit late. Oh, Sunday, I think I told you, Mother wants to go to Greenville to see her sister, so I'll be gone until about dark tomorrow."

She got up and I looked at her as she retrieved her

clothes, slipping first into the little cotton panties. God, I loved looking at her.

She turned to me as we both finished dressing, "Now those dishes, Mr. Lover Boy. They're not going to do themselves."

"But you're not going to do anything about them. I'll have them done and my desk restored before you drive back to Manteo."

"Just let me . . ."

"No."

She made a trip to the bathroom and when she came back out I made her promise to call me when she got home.

At close to nine she still hadn't called, and I was about to call her when the phone rang. I picked up before the first ring ended. It was Elly. She sounded a little breathless.

"Sorry I didn't call right away . . . I had to calm down Lauren's mother and have a little talk with Martin."

"What's up?"

"Shortly after I left to come over to your house, Martin and Lauren saw a puppy and chased it out toward the road. From what I gather from Martin and from Lauren's mother, a man driving by stopped his car and asked if they were lost. They were all the way out to the road, apparently. According to Lauren, the man—and they didn't know who he was— asked them if they wanted a ride back home."

I tried to make it sound innocent. "Maybe it was just a neighbor."

She said she didn't think so. "They know they're not supposed to go to the end of our little road. Anyway, when the man spoke to them—he was in a big car, Martin said— Martin grabbed Lauren's hand and they ran back to our yard."

"A little hero," I said, trying to make it sound light.

"Mother said she brought Martin in. When I got home, Mother was on the phone with Lauren's mother . . . again. I talked to her, too. She gets pretty excited. They both know

now—Martin and Lauren—puppies or not, they're not supposed to leave the yard."

"Probably was nothing, Elly."

"I know, I know. Just the same . . . I guess we're all
haunted by you know what."

"Understandable," I said. "But Martin won't talk to
strangers." I chuckled, still trying. "Heck, he'll hardly talk to
me."

Her voice got easier, and she returned my chuckle.

When we said goodnight and ended the telephone call, I
stood there a moment thinking about the Luanne Wright
thing. Couldn't help it. It was only natural.

Then I turned and began clearing the table, doing the
dishes, and trying not to think. Just the same, I knew there
was still someone out there somewhere. Someone evil.

Chapter Fifteen

As an investigative reporter and crime writer, I've learned over the years a very useful tool: That is, take the accepted scenario—the conventional wisdom—turn it around and look at it from the opposite angle. If such-and-such is what everyone seems to think, just suppose they are all wrong. Assume that they are. Look at it that way.

On the Luanne Wright case, the accepted theory was that this act was done by a stranger to the Outer Banks; someone just passing through.

But what if that was all wrong? Suppose, just suppose, that it was done by someone who lived on the Outer Banks—but went elsewhere to commit similar crimes. And had done so for years.

That was the supposition I decided to pursue, especially since the traditional thinking was paying no dividends.

So on Saturday, I hunkered down with my computer and began searching the Internet. The project: checking the Internet concerning missing young girls.

Basically, I cast out a net for information on lost or missing girls between six and ten years of age reported in North and South Carolina and Virginia. As the flood of results came in, I narrowed the search to Tidewater Virginia and Eastern North Carolina. That file was more manageable. Still a depressing number. Some were listed as runaways—the older ones—and a number had been reported abducted by relatives, estranged spouses, that sort of thing.

I kept narrowing my search, and reading reports and pleas from distressed parents and relatives seeking information. No, not the happiest kind of reading.

Most of the results I was getting were fairly current. Broadening the time period, but keeping the search fairly close to the Outer Banks, I included any reported cases going back twenty years. Spent some time weeding through those. The earliest one I found was eighteen years ago. This one was in the little town of Nashville, North Carolina, near Rocky Mount. Two years later there was one in Corapeake, near the border between North Carolina and Virginia, just south of Suffolk, Virginia.

None of these girls were recovered, nor were their bodies ever found.

After a while I had to get up and stretch. Got a cup of coffee and went out on the deck to breath in some fresh air off the ocean. Another beautiful day. Glancing at my watch, I saw the morning was slipping away and I went back inside and plopped down at the computer. Continued my search.

Shortly after eleven o'clock, I came across two fairly recent ones that were most interesting. Both abductions occurred in or on the outskirts of Rocky Mount, about a two-and-a-half hour drive from the Outer Banks. One was only eighteen months ago, and the other was a bit more than two years earlier.

The earlier one was a girl of eight. In the later one, the girl was almost ten. And the latest one's body was found. There had to be newspaper articles about that. I checked the archives of *The News & Observer*, Raleigh's paper. Yep, three articles about the discovery of the body, plus some background that was most useful.

And the thing I found most hopeful was the name of the lead detective on both of the cases—Don Quinton. Two years earlier I had worked with him on a crime article, not

involving either of these two missing girls. We had gotten
along well. He was a real professional and dedicated lawman. In my records I was sure I had his phone number, or at
least the number of the detective bureau.

Quickly, I found the number and called. As expected, a
dispatcher answered. I identified myself and asked for Don
Quinton.

"He's not in," the dispatcher said in a bored monotone.

"Would you do something for me then?" I said.

He waited.

"Would you please call him and ask him to call me
when he gets a chance?" I gave him my name again, spelled
it for him, and repeated my number.

Again the bored monotone: "What's this regarding?"

"I'm a writer and he and I worked on a story a couple of
years ago, and I want to talk with him about another case."

The dispatcher sounded a bit more interested. "Okay, I'll
call him, Mr. Harrison, and give him the message."

"It's Weaver," I said. "Harrison Weaver."

"Right." He made a muffled response to someone in the
background, then spoke into the phone again. "Not sure I can
reach him or that he'll call back, but I'll give him the message."

I thanked him and kept my fingers crossed. Went back
to the articles about the missing girls. One was white, the
other black. The black girl was the one whose body was
found in a shallow grave. She had been dead only a few
days. Her clothing was mostly missing or torn. The newspaper articles declined to say whether she had been sexually
abused, but that was the impression. Apparently, too, she had
been manually strangled.

Thirty minutes later my phone rang. I grabbed it. Don
Quinton said, "What the hell you up to?"

I told him.

"Jesus, Weav, you are wrasslin' with an old one." Quinton was in his early fifties. He was one of those guys who

seemed to stay fit although his most vigorous exercise was probably walking to the soft drink or coffee machine in the break room.

I went into a recap of the results of my Internet search.

"So what are you thinking?" His voice was flat, but edged with genuine curiosity.

I took a breath and said it: "I'm thinking we may have a serial killer out there. And I believe he lives in this area or maybe yours. Nearby, anyway. I believe most of these have been done by the same person."

He was quiet for what seemed like a minute or more. Then he said softly, "That's my feeling exactly." Another pause. Then he went, on, a frustrated edge to his voice. "But we can't seem to get a handle on this bastard. So what next? What's the next step? I don't know. Wait for him to get another little girl? Hope he slips up? And we nab the son of a bitch."

Another pause, thinking apparently how much to say to me. "You're not writing daily news stuff, are you?"

"No. And let me assure you, Don, anything you say . . . you know the drill."

"Got it. Well, yes on the serial thing, but the chief wants me to keep real quiet about any theories along those lines. So far, we've been lucky and the news guys and gals haven't been pursuing that angle. Sort of surprised."

"Yes, me, too." Now it was my time to hesitate a moment. "But, Don, the way these have been progressing—and it looks like from what I've been able to find out—the first one was this one over in Manteo. But . . ."

"Yeah, I know. He's picking up the pace. The cases are getting closer together. We're about ready for another one. Jesus, I hope not. But I've got a bad feeling, and I've alerted some of my fellow detectives in nearby towns. If another one happens, you can bet your ass that the media will be all over it."

"Maybe we can catch him before then," I said.

"Yeah, good luck on that. He's evaded us for a long time."

"Well, just maybe . . ."

"Keep in touch with me you hear anything or anything happens.

"I will. Same on your end."

We ended the call. I sat there a few minutes. Thinking. Even before talking with Detective Don Quinton I was pretty much convinced we had a serial killer. That Luanne Wright was not the only one.

Now I was more certain.

And possibly the bastard was right here at the Outer Banks.

Chapter Sixteen

On Monday morning, I headed up to Southern Shores to see Harvey Mitchell. He was scheduled to be back at the local bank after visiting bank branches at the end of last week when I tried to see him.

Don't ask what I expected to find out, for I had no idea; just wanted to see someone not connected with the family, one of the lead volunteers, who spent many, many hours searching for Luanne Wright. See what he had to say about the experience. I planned to do the same with Devon Sasser and a few other volunteers. Quite frankly, I didn't hold out much hope for anything revealing, but looking into this case, these were necessary—if not necessarily fruitful—steps that needed to be taken.

Too, I wanted to be as objective in my opinion of Harvey Mitchell as I could. Mabel's apparent dislike of him I knew would weigh on my view and I was determined to try not to let it color my personal take. Good luck, right?

I had done a bit of background on Mitchell. I knew he had been married and divorced twice and was currently married to a woman four years his elder, one of the principal stockholders in the bank. Well, success is success.

As it so happened, Harvey Mitchell was in the lobby, leaning an elbow on one of the tall glass-topped tables that contained slots for deposit slips and other documents, including a couple of brochures about the wonderful features this particular bank offered prospective customers. He was finishing up a conversation with an elderly man in khakis and plaid shirt.

Harvey Mitchell appeared to be in his mid-fifties, thickening a bit in the middle but erect and fit looking. He could easily be considered handsome. His full head of light brown hair had a great deal of gray; it was brushed to one side with a neat part on the left.

He straightened up from the table and shook the customer's hand as they parted. I stood back a few paces. As the elderly man left, Mitchell turned to me, a big smile of welcome on his face, gray-blue eyes twinkling, his wire-framed glasses catching some of the overhead light.

"Hello, Mr. Weaver. Welcome. Hope you're here to open an account with us."

I was only mildly surprised that he knew who I was. A couple or so high-profile cases had thrown me into some prominence in the county; that plus the fact that one of my books had been turned into a TV movie. "Good to see you, Mr. Mitchell. Lovely bank." I glanced around approvingly. It was bright and airy, very modern. But I avoided saying anything about opening an account.

"Please, it's Harvey, not Mr. Mitchell."

"And there's no 'mister' with my name either. Just Weav is fine."

"Come on in my office and tell me what you're up to—chasing crime stories . . . or whatever." He led me to his glass-fronted office just off the lobby, with its view of the lobby. He sat behind his large desk and I took the comfortable chair in front, my narrow reporter's notebook in my hand. His friendly smile seemed perpetual.

"Actually," I said, "I'm not exactly chasing a crime story, but to tell you the truth, Harvey, I have become fascinated with a very old story here in the county—a story that's more than two decades old."

He trained those blue-gray eyes on me and the smile continuing, maybe with a tinge of expectation creeping in. "I'll bet I know which one that is." He bobbed his head a couple of times. "The little girl, the Wright girl, who went missing. Leigh Anne or something Wright." The smile broadened.

"Yes. Luanne Wright." I was determined to return his smile. "I believe you were active in the search party. You were mentioned in at least one of the newspaper stories." I flipped open my notebook and pretended to be checking names.

"Oh, yes, I was active. My whole Rotary Club was. In fact, I guess we had a real cross-section of the county involved. White and black citizens. Everybody. We were united. It was an all-out effort." He shook his head. "But we never turned up anything. Just like she'd vanished off the face of the earth." He kept his eyes on me for the most part, but I noticed that every time someone moved past in the lobby—especially a female—he briefly glanced in that direction, and then back at me. "Tell me why you're interested in this case, this really old case? I thought you mostly wrote about what's happening in the present day."

"I was talking with my friend Chief Deputy Odell Wright, the girl's older brother. He welcomed my taking a look at the old file. See if I saw anything new. It is a fascinating case, and a very tragic one, one that still haunts Deputy Wright and probably many others."

Mitchell nodded agreement. "Poor Odell. He was just a youngster then. Heck, so was I. Not as young as Odell, though, who was only about eighteen or nineteen I guess. He was there on the search every day. So was his daddy. But Odell hung out at the courthouse for weeks afterwards. I guess, hoping for a positive development." Mitchell removed his glasses and held them up to the light for inspection. He wiped at the lens vigorously with a small purple cloth from his top middle drawer, and put the glasses aside.

With hardly more than a smile of encouragement from me, Mitchell continued: "The late Sheriff Claxton helped personally, too. In fact, he took Odell under his wing, so to speak." He toyed with his glasses a moment, moving them back and forth on his desktop with the fingertips of one hand. "I believe Sheriff Claxton is the one who encouraged Odell to get a degree, an associate degree I guess it was, in law enforcement, or criminal justice, and join the Sheriff's Department. He's been there ever since. Doing quite well I understand."

"Yes, he has done well. He's made Chief Deputy," I said. Then, "Tell me about the search, your impression of it, what you saw, what you didn't see, and anything you can remember about it."

He said, "Well, it was a long time ago. More than twenty years. But I remember we searched all over the island—and beyond. We went up and down along the waterfronts, all around the whole island, I guess, at one time or another." He gave his head a slight shake. "This went on for days, and much of it was in the rain. In the woods, we formed a line and advanced in, I guess, military style." This time he gave his head a pronounced shake. "Nothing. Never a scrap of anything."

I glanced at my notebook again. "How long did the search—the full search—go on?"

"Let me think now." He touched the earpieces of his glasses again. "It had to have been several days, maybe a week. I mean when there were dozens of us involved. I know the rain had stopped, and it had lasted for about four days." He glanced at a woman and small child who passed in the lobby; then back at me. "Of course, there wasn't the full group of searchers after that. The numbers began to dwindle, as you can imagine." He went into more detail about the search; about how a coffee and doughnut stand had been set up for the volunteers; and how a general frustration had developed as the days passed without any success. His expression had become more serious, the smile disappearing, as he recounted those days.

When he mentioned the coffee and doughnuts, I of course thought about Estelle Byerly.

When he paused, as if he had finished, I leaned forward a bit. "What's your theory, Harvey, as to what happened to her?"

He gave a mirthless little chuckle. "Of course, someone grabbed her. Took her. Did heaven knows what to her, and I'm sure killed her eventually, if not right away."

"What's your theory as to who did this? Any thoughts along those lines?"

He didn't hesitate. "I go along with what most of us began to believe, and that is that it had to be a stranger. Don't want to say tourist, but that's the most likely."

I nodded. "I believe that's what . . ." and I paused long enough to refer to my notepad. ". . . I believe that's what one of the searchers, Devon Sasser was quoted in the newspaper as speculating."

At the mention of Devon Sasser, a quick expression flickered across his face. I couldn't decipher what it was. But the name registered some feeling with him. "Oh, yes, that was the sentiment of most of us I'm sure," Mitchell said.

I went back to my notes. "You, Devon Sasser, Herschel Creef, Samuel Midgette, and two or three others were mentioned in different newspaper account and in some of the reports as being leaders in the search."

"Well, I'm not sure we were what you'd call leaders. But we were there from the beginning and were quite involved."

"Many of these folks still around?" I showed him a page in the notebook where I had jotted down seven names, including his.

Leaning forward to view the notepad that I extended toward him, he retrieved his glasses and put them on. "I can tell you right off that Herschel Creef died about five years ago, Midgette is still here in real estate down in Nags Head. Devon Sasser is still around—off and on. I think he has a traveling job, sales or something. The others there, these two have moved, and this one—Mel Stevens—I don't know. Don't remember him."

"Thank you," I said. "I may check with Mr. Midgette . . ."

"He'll try to sell you a new house." Mitchell chuckled.

I tried to be somewhat jovial in return. "Devon Sasser. Maybe he's in the phone book." I knew, of course, that he was.

"Oh, I think he still lives here. At least part of the time. Not trying to spread rumors, but I remember he and his wife were splitting up about the time we were doing the searching." He raised his eyebrows and tilted his head to one side. "I think she sort of went off the deep end."

I looked at him questioningly. "From what I understand, that's when she became the 'Bear Woman.'" From what Mabel had indicated to me, Harvey Mitchell may have been responsible for that split-up between Estelle and Devon. But Mitchell's expression remained neutral, hidden mostly by that perpetual smile.

I decided to go ahead and confront Mitchell with what I had heard. "I don't mean to embarrass you, Harvey, in any way, but weren't you and Estelle Byerly Sasser very . . . very close at that time?

His expression became steely, even though the smile remained. "Do you mean were we having an affair? That's pretty common knowledge, but that was a long, long time ago and I completely lost touch with her when she moved out to the woods." Then his eyes bore into me, and the smile was gone. "But what's that got to do with the case you're investigating?"

"No, you're absolutely right, Harvey, it doesn't have a direct bearing on the case but I was just curious why a woman like that would suddenly move into the woods . . . forever."

His expression softened somewhat. "She was a beautiful woman then, and she and Sasser were not getting along. But no, I was not responsible for her deciding to move to the woods. I think that was to get away from Sasser."

I nodded and then mumbled something like: "Sorry. Didn't mean to stray off into something not bearing directly on the case."

"No problem," he said, that smile, somewhat forced, pasted across his face. Then he consulted an appointment calendar in front of him. "That's about all I know . . . or re-member," he said.

His body language told me he wanted to end the interview.

In just another moment, a strikingly attractive young woman in her early twenties tapped on the door and came into the office. She wore a rather low-cut blouse of a silk-like material and a short skirt. She was a knockout. As she entered, she said, "Excuse me for interrupting, Mr. Mitchell, but you have this message that I thought you should have."

Mitchell took the slip of paper she handed across the desk. I couldn't help but cast a quick look at her cleavage. He nodded. "Thank you, Denise. Yes, I need to take care of this."

I don't know what the signal was, but I have done enough interviews to know that in some fashion Mitchell had signaled Denise to interrupt the conference, bring him a note that needed "immediate attention." Maybe it was when he fumbled with his appointment calendar. Made no difference. We had finished anyway.

I gave him one of my cards. "I appreciate your talking with me about that, that tragedy and the search involved. And, it goes almost without saying, but if anything occurs to you that might be helpful—after all these years—I'd appreci-ate a call, and I know Odell would appreciate it."

He took my card and slipped it into his top drawer, where I knew it would stay—unused.

Chapter Seventeen

Leaving the bank, I sat in my car for a minute or so before I started the engine and drove the short distance to Market Place Shopping Center and parked near the bagel shop. Figured maybe a cup of strong black coffee was in order. I got the coffee and went outside and sat at one of the little tables, staring off across the parking area, watching people go by—and wondering what in the hell I expected to find out talking with Harvey Mitchell or anyone else involved in a fruitless search for a little girl more than twenty years ago. Except that I knew deep down what I was doing: I was getting a feel for the personality of someone who was there during the search. Was I looking for a local suspect? I tried not to let myself think too optimistically along those lines. Just the same, I knew myself well enough to know that I didn't really feel like I was truly wasting my time.

At the same time, I didn't want to unduly raise hope in Odell's heart that something might come of it. Was it ego on my part, thinking I could make a difference? Perhaps see something that trained lawmen and others hadn't seen over the years? Get real, Weaver. Get real.

My coffee was getting cold. And so was my enthusiasm for hoping I might make a difference in a twenty-two-year-old case. Nonetheless, as Elly said, I was like a dog with a bone. I wasn't going to let it go.

Getting in my car, I drove south to Kill Devil Hills and down to Bay Drive and Devon Sasser's address I had looked up. No luck. No one was there. Off traveling with his job, I assumed.

I went home and made a couple of fruitless calls to some of the other searchers I had on my list. Finally, though, I did get through to Samuel Midgette. He was pleasant and wanted to interest me in some prime real estate. I told him why I was calling. He was willing to talk—for a minute or two, and then switched back to real estate sales. Nothing there. He commented about how they turned up nothing. "I'm afraid pursuing this is a really, really lost cause," he said.

I thanked him, and sat there for a while. Then I looked up the number of Harvey Mitchell's branch bank in Rocky Mount. Part of my—what?—perverse nature, which I like to think of as a reporter's instinct, I called the Rocky Mount bank and asked for Harvey Mitchell, knowing full well of course he was here at the Outer Banks.

A very professional sounding woman answered.

I identified myself. "I'm trying to reach Harvey Mitchell," I said.

"Sorry but he's at the home office in Kitty Hawk," she said.

"Oh," I said. "I thought he might still be there in Rocky Mount. I understand he went there the end of the week."

The woman hesitated. "No sir, Mr. Weaver. He wasn't here. He won't be here for another week or so."

I thanked her and hung up. Got more than I expected. But puzzling. Sometimes my reporter's instincts pay off. Or is it my perverse nature?

So I called Detective Don Quinton at the Rocky Mount police department. Surprisingly, he answered when I was switched to the detective bureau.

"Didn't expect to hear from you so soon" he said. "You got a lead on something?"

I assured him I didn't but that I was curious about the

activities of one of the persons who had been active in the initial search for Luanne Wright years ago.

Then I related, as delicately as I could, that this outstanding citizen was reported to have been at the bank's branch there in Rocky Mount last week, but he hadn't been.

"I'm curious where he might have been. If he was even in Rocky Mount." I added, "I know it's a helluva long shot, but I wondered if in that great amount of spare time that you must have if you or one of your colleagues could find out whether he was there and what he was doing."

"Jesus, Weav, you *are* asking a lot," Quinton said. Then, "He a person of interest?"

"Honestly, I don't think so. Certainly not yet. But I'd like to know why the home office thinks one thing—and that ain't the truth."

Quinton was quiet for several moments. I wasn't sure but what he was going to tell me he was too busy. That quip about "spare time" was a myth—that he knew and so did I. Detectives always had more on their plate than they could handle.

"Okay, Weav," he said finally. "So happens I've got a niece who's a teller at that bank and I know a couple of other angles." He permitted himself to sound a bit more upbeat. "Wouldn't it be something if all this nosing around really paid off. That we could nail somebody."

"Don't get your hopes up," I said.

"I'm a twenty-year veteran in police work. I know better'n get my hopes up."

He promised to call.

Who knows? Just maybe.

Tuesday I made a few more calls to people on my list of searchers. Actually talked with a two of them, but to no real avail. Like everyone else, they were of the opinion that it had to be a stranger to the area.

I didn't really think so. Not sure when my opinion began to change and firm up, but I knew it had something to do with where Odell and I both think she was abducted. I mean that was a rather remote area off the beaten path that a tourist would normally have been taking. It had to be someone who knew Luanne would probably have been taking that route home. The abductor lay in wait.

Shortly after lunch, the phone rang and I figured it would be a callback from one of the searchers I had left a message for. But glancing at the phone's ID, I saw it was Rocky Mount police department.

When I answered, Detective Don Quinton said, "Well, your outstanding citizen Mr. Harvey Mitchell is a very busy man."

"Yes?"

"Seems he has a young lady friend in a nice secluded apartment here in town." He gave a short chuckle. "She keeps him pretty busy, I 'spect, when he's here in town."

I was quiet a moment. Perhaps with nothing else to comment on immediately, I said, "So what do you think, Don?"

A sigh was audible. "Probably same as you do, Weav. As a possible 'person of interest,' he doesn't really interest me." As I remember Quinton and one of his mannerisms, I could picture him cocking one eyebrow. "That is unless you got something else."

"No, I don't," I said.

Then he said the same thing I was thinking: "As for young women, yes. But for little girls, no."

"Agreed," I said. "More of a womanizer with a very healthy appetite. But not a child abductor . . . the two don't go together."

"This was all very discreet," Quinton said. "Your good citizen will never know we were checking on him."

"Thanks so very much, Don. I'll keep you posted."

We signed off.

Sometimes as a reporter, you find out things you'd just as soon not know.

Chapter Eighteen

By eleven Wednesday morning I had packed my bass fiddle in its black canvas bag, and it lay on the living room floor ready to go. I wasn't sure whether I'd eaten an early lunch or a very late breakfast but I was no longer hungry and knew I would be okay until dinnertime. I went out on the deck and enjoyed the sun and blue sky. Another lovely day in May. I listened carefully, as I often did, and I was sure I could hear the surf, a quarter of a mile away. If I were honest, I'd admit to myself that most days I couldn't really hear the surf. But when the traffic on the Bypass was light and the tide was high with a northeast wind I could indeed actually hear the ocean. And smell it. A light tinge of salt. After we played today, I vowed to stop by the ocean and spiritually drink it in.

Shortly after twelve, I carried my bass down the outside stairs and stowed it in the back of the Subaru. I chuckled to myself at the realization that each year the bass seemed to get heavier and heavier. Less than twenty minutes later I had pulled into the parking area in Duck at the back of Scarborough Faire behind the Island Bookstore. I unloaded the bass and carried it to the platform on the deck where we would play. Jim Watson was already there and so was Paul Settlemyer setting up his keyboard. Dane Kirchner, our drummer, struggled with his cases. He had more work to getting set up than the rest of us did.

I had unzipped the cover for my bass when Tom Stevens, the trombone player arrived. Jim introduced us all. I shook Tom's hand.

Jim chuckled, "You guys know you're not supposed to shake hands on the bandstand. It's an old chestnut, I know, but we don't want the audience to think you've not been playing together for years and years."

Jim brought stands and his large binders with our single-sheet scores: one for me, one for himself, one for Tom, and one for Paul. Our library of music was what is referred to as "fake books." The melody line is written out and the corresponding chords are printed above the line of the melody. It is the chord chart that I'm most interested in. Unless I do fill-in with a sort of walking bass, which I like to do, I can usually get by playing the root and fifth of the chord.

There were already a smattering of people sitting on benches or milling about waiting for us to start playing. Precisely at one o'clock, Jim kicked off our theme, "A Foggy Day." The tune swung along real upbeat. With Jim on trumpet, Tom on trombone, and Paul on piano, some solid bass, and tasty drumming by Dane, it did sound good, and we got a nice round of applause when we finished. Next we did a slow blues riff in B-flat that Paul, Jim and I had worked out earlier. It went well, too. Then we livened things up with Duke Ellington's "Satin Doll," another favorite of mine that's fun to play.

Things went well, and it was fun playing. The sun was out, the weather warm, and I was really beginning to perspire. Heck, I was beginning to sweat. After the first hour, we took a short break. On longer jobs I usually brought a high stool I can perch on as I play. Today it was all standing, the bass snugged into my side. I laid my bass carefully on its side and sat for a couple of minutes on the bench in front of Island Bookstore. I planned to go in the store when we finished. They had ordered a book for me.

After our short break, we opened with another favorite

of mine that I thought at one time I would never feel comfortable playing again. The tune was Irving Berlin's "Cheek to Cheek." My late wife Keely did a marvelous job performing this song with some of the groups with which the two of us played, and I associated the song so strongly with her that it took me a while after she died before I could play it comfortably. Now I enjoyed the fun chord changes of the melody and I thought about good times of the past, not the death-dealing depression Keely fell into.

Jim played the melody in the lower register. Sounded great. I knew the tune so well that, rather than the usual bass part, I played along with him in unison. Paul gave me a big grin and winked his approval. When we finished the first chorus Jim tilted his head back to me and said, "Take it." With Paul filing in lightly with chords on the keyboard I did the melody solo for the first half, and then Jim and Tom came in on the bridge and we played together on the last eight. We did the chorus one more time and I played the traditional bass part. The crowd gave us a nice round of applause when we finished.

Jim called up one tune after the other. Very little slack time in between. We had a good crowd listening to us. At three o'clock, we signed off and Jim announced that we would be followed by a rollicking bluegrass group. The musicians for the bluegrass band had arrived and they, too, gave us a nice hand. As we quickly packed up to make room for the others, Jim told us "checks would be in the mail." We knew they would be. I put my bass in its cover and carried it to the Subaru. I could swear that it was even heavier than it was early that day. With a small towel in the trunk of the car, I wiped my face and neck. Then I locked the car and went into Bill Rickman's Island Bookstore.

Meaghan, one of the managers at the bookstore, had ordered for me a copy of Patricia C. Click's *Time Full of Trial*, the story of the Freedmen's Colony on Roanoke Island from 1862 to 1867. After talking with Odell Wright about the fact that his little sister had done a paper on what she and others described as "The Other Lost Colony," I wanted to read more about the settlement.

Entering the bookstore, I breathed in deeply. Love the familiar, delightfully overwhelming aroma of a bookstore. The ink, the paper, the books themselves. I could open a new book and smell it with pleasure. It was almost visceral. Too, the bookstore was air-conditioned and that felt good.

Meaghan was at the Kitty Hawk store. A young woman named Kristi waited on me and retrieved my copy of the book from under the counter. A sticky note with my name on it was affixed to the book. I thanked her, paid for it, declined a bag and got ready to walk out, but first I had to browse around a bit. I always felt good in a bookstore. Next to sitting and watching the ocean, a bookstore was my favorite place to be.

Before I left, Kristi said, "You all sounded real good."

"Thanks. It was fun." I hadn't realized she knew I was with the band.

Outside I listened to the bluegrass group for several tunes. They were good. A young woman played upright bass. Her bass was amplified and it came through strongly as she played root and fifth of the traditional three chords on most of the melodies. I applauded, spoke to the woman bass player, and headed for my car and home.

But I vowed to keep the promise to myself and stop by the ocean on my way home. When I got down to the intersection at the end of Duck Road, I made a left onto the Beach Road and parked at the unloading area just below Hilton Garden Inn. I would only be there a few minutes. I walked up to the deck overlooking the beach and the mighty Atlantic. A few people were out on the beach: a young couple with two small children; a woman with a plastic bag in her hand hunting for shells or sea glass. She would bend over every few steps and peer at the brown sand, maybe pick up something, discard it, move on; a man and woman strolled

up the beach. A gentle breeze came from the northeast. The
sky was clear and Carolina Blue. I looked out at the ocean,
how it changed colors near the horizon.

The sheer majesty of the ocean had its effect. I felt
calmed and reverent. Watching the swells and surf, listening
to the sound, gave me a spiritual sense. I always felt, this is
where we came from.

I got home a little before five. After lugging my bass up the
outside stairs and struggling it into the living room. I took
the cover off, stowed the cover in the closet, and actually put
the bass upright in its stand rather than laying it on its side in
the middle of the living room floor.

I spoke to Janey, then sat in the one easy chair and started right in on Patricia Click's book about the Freedmen's
Colony. I read until close to six. Janey wanted to know why
things were so quiet, so I turned on the radio to the classical
station, but I knew she wanted something livelier than what
was playing at the moment, so I switched to 102.5 and got
some rock. She bobbed her head up and down. She didn't
have the beat, but she had the enthusiasm.

Shortly after six I called Elly. She said, "How did the
playing go?"

"Oh, we played pretty. We really did."

"How was the new trombone player?"

"He played very tastefully. A good complement to Jim's
trumpet. And Dane played well on drums. Didn't drown anyone out. In fact, he used brushes on one of the few slow
pieces we played. Of course, Paul is always excellent on
piano . . . keyboard in this instance."

Then I asked her about tomorrow night. We agreed we'd
actually go to a movie. A movie was playing at the Pioneer
Theater in Manteo that reviews said was good. I pronounced
the family-owned Pioneer the way the late H. A. Creef used
to as "thee-ATE-er." He used to give a good telephone-re-

corded synopsis of the movie being shown that night, and what time the one-show-a-night would be over so parents could pick up their children. The theater was my favorite. Old-timey. Refreshments at the small concession stand were reasonable, too. No home mortgages needed to purchase popcorn or a soda.

After we said goodnight, I decided on dinner. I would again make one of my World Famous Salads. But tonight I went all out on it. I used two different kinds of lettuce and some maché, along with cubed ham and turkey, three kinds of cheese, chopped celery, a few walnuts, and small tomato chunks. I topped it with my World Famous Dressing. Well, actually, it wasn't really . . . oh, never mind. When I finished making the huge salad, it was not exactly low-calorie, but it was tasty. And I ate saltine crackers along with the salad. Nothing fancy for crackers. Just saltines. They were the best.

I took the finished salad over to the coffee table. I sat on the sofa and spread a small dishtowel on the floor between the coffee table and my feet. Just in case. Wanted to be careful, too, of the book about the Freedmen's Colony, which I carried with me to read while I ate. Always like to keep my books in good shape—no greasy spots, coffee spills, that sort of thing.

While reading, I kept forgetting to eat. Fascinating story. The colony, which at one time at its height, had about three thousand former slaves, with housing, dirt roads, a school and churches, lasted only five years, from 1862 to 1867. There are absolutely no remains of the Freedmen's Colony left today on Roanoke Island. For that reason, I thought the title of the paper Luanne Wright had written as well as a piece on the Internet I printed out to go along with Professor Click's tome was so appropriate. The article by Kathleen Angione was published in the 2005 issue of *Coastwatch* and titled "The Freemen of Roanoke Island: The Other Lost Colony." The idea of another Lost Colony, in addition to the ill-fated effort by Sir Walter Raleigh to establish a permanent English colony on Roanoke Island in 1587, was a perfect title.

In 1862, Union forces captured the Confederate fortifycations on Roanoke Island, and almost immediately former slaves began to arrive on the island from the mainland so they could be near the Union military. Soon the camp with the former slaves became more than just a refuge; under guidance and supervision by the Reverend Horace James, a Congregational chaplain, the Roanoke Freedmen's Colony began to flourish. James envisioned the Roanoke Island colony as a model for resettlement of other freedmen after the war.

After President Abraham Lincoln's Emancipation Proclamation, even more former slaves—men, women, and children—continued flooding onto Roanoke Island. They built one-room cabins, roads, schools and churches. By and large, the education, social work, and other help was carried out by representatives, mostly women, of the American Missionary Association. The freedmen (referred to in the beginning as "contraband") tried farming and even a sawmill, all in an effort to become self-sufficient.

As the war ended, however, so did the Freedmen's Colony on Roanoke Island. President Andrew Johnson issued his Amnesty Proclamation in 1865, returning all property seized by Union forces to the original owners. This meant that the land for the Freedmen's Colony, as well as other camps throughout the South, went back to the original white owners.

By 1867, the Freedmen's Colony on Roanoke Island was abandoned. Most of the former residents of the colony had left the island by that time. The 1870 census recorded only three hundred blacks living on Roanoke Island.

But today, a few of the blacks living on Roanoke Island are descendants of those first Freedmen. As Odell Wright told me, he is one of the descendants. After much research, he'd traced his ancestry back to his great-grandmother, who came from the mainland during the war and was one of those original residents of "The Other Lost Colony."

It was close to midnight when I finished reading. I realized the salad plate still sat in front of me on the coffee table. I got up and stretched my back, feeling the stiffness in my body from having sat so long. I took the plate to the kitchen sink, and covered Janey's cage. Well past her bed-time. Mine, too.

But I stood at the sink staring out at the night, thinking about what I had read—about the Freedmen's Colony and the link Odell and his family had to those early people on the island. There was in me now even more of a desire to unravel the mystery surrounding little Luanne Wright's disappearance. I felt like I owed an obligation to her, and to all the others. We didn't need still another "lost" soul. My obsession—and that's what it had become—was even stronger to unravel the mystery surrounding the disappearance of Luanne Wright.

Chapter Nineteen

The phone rang shortly after seven-thirty Thursday morning. I stood in the kitchen, enjoying the view through the window, and had just taken the first sip of coffee. I looked across the room and frowned at the phone, wrinkling my brow. Why we do that, I don't know. It's as if the inanimate object has come alive and done something to annoy us.

With coffee mug in hand, I went from the kitchen across the living room to the phone. I didn't have to step over the neck of the bass fiddle since I had actually put it in its stand the afternoon before.

I could see by the caller ID that it was Balls' cell number.

"Well, good morning," I said. I could hear road noise.

"Yeah, good morning to you," he grumbled.

I knew Balls was not calling because all was at peace in the world. That wasn't his style.

So he lowered the boom, as I knew he would: "There's been a body found in the woods over beyond Mann's Harbor. It's the Bear Woman."

"Oh, Christ," I muttered.

"Yeah, you're gonna have Schweikert all over you again. You pay a visit to someone. A few days later they turn up dead."

Rick Schweikert was the district attorney. He didn't like

me. The feeling was pretty much mutual. It dated from an unflattering piece I wrote about him three or four years ago, describing him as a pompous, arrogant ass. The article was accurate. Ever since, he's claimed I'm a magnate for dead bodies, and he'd love to pin something on me.

I couldn't believe the woman I had seen just a week before was dead. "What?" I said. "What happened?"

"First report I got, by way of Odell, is that it looks like the bears turned on her."

I know there was puzzlement in my tone. "After twenty years, the bears suddenly turn on her?"

"That's why they called me. Got a make sure it was the bears . . ." Then he added with a chuckle, ". . . and not you."

"Not funny, Balls. It really makes me . . . makes me sad to hear about it. I mean, she was not all that nice to me when I was there, but she surely seemed to be content doing what she'd been doing for years." I thought about what she had been busy with when I arrived. "Heck, she was planting a little vegetable garden beside her trailer."

A more somber Balls: "Finding a body is never a happy thing." And just that quick his voice changed. Businesslike, but more like Balls. "I'm about ten minutes from your place. You can go with me—if you promise to buy me lunch or dinner or something afterwards."

I agreed of course. And I thought, what a way to spend a lovely spring morning: going to look at a body. The body of a woman with whom I had talked only a week earlier.

I finished my coffee, grabbed a bagel for the toaster. Checked to make sure Janey had sufficient seeds and fresh-enough water. She bobbed her head at me. "Okay, Janey," I said, "I'll give you a little sprig of millet." I was finishing the bagel when I heard the deep, throaty rumble of Balls' classic old Thunderbird pull into my cul-de-sac.

I hurried downstairs and squeezed into the passenger side. I took a quick look at him. The bandage was gone from his forehead. Two-inch reddish scar above his left eyebrow.

"You're healing nicely," I said.

"Yeah." Nothing else.

He pulled forward and headed up to the Bypass. Wasting no time, he wormed right into the light traffic flow and headed south.

I handed him one of the two high-energy granola bars I snatched from the kitchen as I came out. He made a face. "Thanks," he said, "but you still got a buy me lunch or dinner or something."

"What's the story on the body?" I said.

"One of the people lives in the woods near there found her this morning. Said it looked like one of the bears turned on her."

"Awfully early in the morning to be finding a body."

Balls shrugged.

I thought about the rutty road to her place in the woods. "You taking your car out there?"

"No way," he said. "We're meeting Odell at the courthouse. "Going in one of the department's off-road vehicles." He moved deftly around two slower cars in front of us. "One of the deputies is already out there."

We were quiet a minute or two. He was already close to Whalebone Junction, ready to swing right toward Manteo. I said, "She wasn't too popular, you know, with some of those neighbors lived out there not too far from her."

"That's what I'd heard." The Balls chuckle again. "Threatened to send a load of buckshot their way if they didn't get off her property, leave her bears alone." Then he added, "I got a see some of those good ol' boys anyway. Another matter."

I knew he referred to his suspicion—or maybe knowledge—that some of those 'good ol' boys' were dealing drugs, maybe producing them or growing some weed.

We were crossing the long Washington Baum Bridge over Roanoke Sound, starting on the high uprise. Balls glanced over at me. "Odell'll be waiting for us. You won't have time to slip in there and see your sweetie."

Now it was my turn to shrug. I didn't bother to say anything.

As we parked in a reserved spot at the courthouse, Balls unwrapped his granola bar. He looked around for a place to deposit the wrapper, didn't see one, and wadded the paper up and stuck it in the side pocket of his lightweight windbreaker. He stuffed half the bar in his mouth and chomped away loudly. Deputy Odell Wright stood by the open driver's door of the off-road vehicle, and he motioned for us. Balls got in the front passenger's seat and I slipped into the back, moving a large digital Canon camera over to the side of the seat.

Odell shook Balls' hand and nodded back toward me as he turned the ignition on and started away from the courthouse and downtown Manteo.

We were on our way to go look at a body that had probably been killed by a bear several days ago. It wouldn't be pretty.

And Balls was worried about lunch or dinner.

I wasn't hungry.

Chapter Twenty

Rather than swing east and loop around to take the new Virginia Dare Memorial Bridge over Croatan Sound, Odell stayed west on Highway 64 toward the old Mann's Harbor Bridge. We went past the airport road near where Elly lives, and past what was the mini-estate of the late actor Andy Griffith and then Fort Raleigh and the site of The Lost Colony.

Odell drove fast, but he didn't have his light bar on. I looked at the side of his face and thought about how he had been studying that old case file earlier in the week. He was all business, concentrating on his driving.

Balls, his eyes straight ahead, said, "Fill me in."

"Deputy Dorsey is there on site," Odell said. "He has secured the area. Made sure nothing was moved. Medics are there or on their way. The sheriff alerted Dr. Willis and he's on his way, also."

"Person who notified the department?"

"Citizen named Wyatt Wilkinson. Dorsey says he's keeping him close by." Odell glanced briefly at Balls and then back at the road. "Dorsey says the body is decomposing, and messed up quite a bit. Probably dead a few days . . . in this heat."

"Yeah," Balls said.

Odell shook his head.

I couldn't help but wonder if he thought what might have happened to his little sister's body all those years ago.

I used the period of relative quiet to fill Odell in on my talk with Harvey Mitchell and a couple of the others. I didn't say anything about Mitchell's arrangement in Rocky Mount with a young woman, or my failed attempt to see Devon Sasser. As the long-ago divorced husband of the Bear Woman I figured his name would come up sooner than later. But I did mention that I had talked with Detective Don Quinton in Rocky Mount about other cases.

Odell just listened. Balls was silent, staring straight ahead.

I was tempted to expound on my theory that maybe it was someone local who abducted Luanne, and not a stranger to the area. But I decided to save that.

We rode without talking through Mann's Harbor and past Stan's Market. When we got closer to East Lake, Odell slowed and peered to the right. We saw the small road, the one I had driven on just about a week ago. I was reminded how it was more of a path than a road. A field was on one side and tall pines and hardwoods, bramble and undergrowth on the other. Carefully, Odell navigated the vehicle onto the deeply rutted path. About fifty yards into the path, the area opened into a field on both sides and the ride became relatively smoother.

Another fifty yards and we saw a Dare County Sheriff's Department vehicle parked to one side of the path. Beyond the vehicle there was a large circle of yellow police tape, strung from tree to tree. Estelle's ratty, falling-down faded green house trailer was partially hidden by woods around it. Beyond the trailer, her older small blue Chevrolet—or at least it had been blue at one time—nosed close to the trailer but inside the circle of tape.

Within the tape was where the body had to be. Deputy Dorsey stood a few yards from his vehicle; another man in jeans and work shirt stood beside him. They turned toward us as we eased to a stop. We got out of the off-road vehicle, and I heard the medics' ambulance lumbering up behind us, going slow, carefully avoiding ruts in the path. The rescue squad stopped near Odell's vehicle but the two medics didn't get out immediately.

Deputy Dorsey was in his twenties, a bit heavy, with closely cropped reddish hair. His face, usually rather florid, was pale. He nodded at Odell and Balls, and swallowed as if bile had risen from his throat. He acknowledged me with the barest duck of his head. He kept his back to the trailer, and what we knew lay there.

Dorsey jerked a thumb at the man beside him. "This here's Wyatt Wilkinson. He lives back over there about a mile or so. He's the one who came up here early this morning and found her."

Wilkinson, whose age was difficult to determine but probably in the range of a hard-lived sixty years, bobbed his head on a scrawny neck, acknowledging what Dorsey had said. "I hadn't seen her in quite a spell. I usually do see her every few days or so. She wandered all over the place, her property and anybody else's she had a mind to." His prominent Adam's apple moving up and down as he spoke.

Dorsey said, "He went back to his place and called it in."

Wilkinson screwed up his mouth. "Tell you the truth, I seen road kill look better'n she does."

Wilkinson obviously caught the expression on my face at his comment. He shrugged, embarrassed, and mumbled, "Didn't mean no disrespect."

Balls looked hard at Wilkinson. "Why'd you come over here this morning?"

Wilkinson shrugged his boney shoulders. "I dunno. I guess I wondered what was up. Tell you the truth, too, I wanted to make sure she won't doing any burning of trash or nothing like she does sometimes. Been so dry, you know. Not enough rain to even lay down the dust."

Balls nodded a dismissal. Then to Odell he said, "Get your deputy to get Mr. Wilkinson's ID, address, and send him on his way. Doesn't need to be hanging around."

I didn't see Wilkinson leave right away. But he must have drifted off at some point. I wasn't concentrating on him.

The two male medics came to where we stood. I recognized one of them, Duncan, who had been driving. Balls gave a quick shake to his head, and they stayed silently in place.

To Odell, Balls said, "Let's take a look." He glanced around. "Rest of you stay here."

We watched them make their way gingerly to the scene. They were careful where they stepped. Balls kept his eyes toward the ground. I could see a lump of something a couple of yards from the door of the trailer. It had to be the body. Balls and Odell stood there looking down. Then Balls knelt for a closer look. He took a handkerchief from his rear pocket and held it over his nose. Odell shook his head. Balls stood again, placing his hand on the small of his back as he straightened up.

Another vehicle approached. It was Dr. Willis' dusty sedan. He pulled in beside the rescue vehicle and laboriously made his way out of the driver's side. Opening the rear door, he extracted his black medical bag, and then stood still for a moment longer. He wore a dress shirt and tie, the tie loosened and the shirt baggy at his waist as if not tucked in properly. He appeared to take a deep breath and then approached the yellow crime scene tape.

Balls saw him and motioned him forward. Dr. Willis, the county's acting corner (and still called the "acting coroner" as he had been for years), lifted the tape and ducked under. But not completely. The tape caught on his right shoulder and he plucked it off with delicate fingers and moved over to Balls and Odell. He looked down at the body and, like Odell, he shook his head. Then he slowly went down on one knee and began to look more closely at the body. Dr.

Willis said something to Balls that I couldn't hear and Balls helped him back to his feet. The rest of us were silent. Very, very quiet. The second medic whispered something to Duncan, and Duncan gave a quick shake of his head and didn't say anything.

The three of them stood inside the yellow tape talking a few minutes, and Balls appeared to agree with whatever it was that Dr. Willis was saying. But Balls held one hand up as if signaling to wait a few minutes. Then he began to take careful, short steps away from the body and surveyed the ground in a semicircle manner for several yards away from the front of the trailer and the body. He came back to Odell and Dr. Willis and said something, a puzzled expression on his face.

Odell apparently agreed with what Balls was saying. Then Odell faced toward the group of us and called out, his voice sounding startlingly loud in the silence that hovered over us, "Dorsey, get the camera out of the back of my vehicle."

Dorsey hesitated just a beat, and I spoke out: "I'll get it. I know where it is."

Dorsey's slight shift in his body signaled relief that he didn't have to trek back over to the body. I scurried over to the off-road cruiser, opened the back door and grabbed the camera. It appeared new and heavier than I thought it would be.

I ducked under the crime scene tape and approached the trio standing near the body. Dr. Willis talked with Balls as I approached with the camera and handed it to Odell. Dr. Willis said, ". . . I can't do much with this body now. Not in the condition it's in. It needs to go over the Greenville, get an autopsy there. But from the looks of it, surely appears the bears turned on her." He shook his head. "Hell, they're wild animals. Wild animals are unpredictable."

Odell began taking pictures from different angles of the body.

At first I avoided looking directly at the remains. But from a quick glance I was oddly reminded of a picture in a *National Geographic* of archeologist uncovering the tomb of a long-ago dead Egyptian. That ancient body was mummified. This one was not, of course. Yet there was something about the finality of the scene that brought that picture to mind.

Being a reporter and writer, there was no way I could not look. I tried flipping that little mental switch I have—and that works sometimes—so that I could attempt to emotionally distance myself from what I was seeing, the remains of a woman I talked with only days ago.

Chapter Twenty-One

And it was as bad as I expected. Holding a handkerchief to my face, I peered momentarily at the body. That was enough. Flesh, though discolored and bloated, was still on the body. The clothes were tattered, dirty. One filthy sneaker was on the right foot; the left foot was bare and at least two of the toes were missing. Arms and legs at strange and unnatural angles, her pants and a ratty shirt almost black with dried blood, her hair across her face. I turned away. I'd seen enough. The sight was etched in my mind in case I ever had to write about it. I stepped away, upwind, and looked up at the tall pine trees and the blue sky and took a deep breath, forcing myself to breathe slowly.

I was having a difficult time remembering Estelle Byerly puttering in her garden when I first saw her. I tried vainly to concentrate on that.

Dr. Willis tugged at the wrist of his latex gloves as if securing them more protectively. He pursed his lips, turned his head toward Balls, then back at the body. "She's got a wound on the back of her head. Whether from a bite from one of the bears—they got powerful jaws—I can't tell, and this left shoulder, what's left of it, shows a great deal of trauma. Chewed on or dragged around, I'm not sure."

Balls nodded. "I understand," he said. "We'll get a few more pictures and then have the medics transport the remains to Greenville." He addressed Odell. "Get some pictures, Odell, around the area of the body. The ground. And up close to where she's been lying. When they move the body, I want pictures of the ground where the body was." He had a puzzled cast to his face. "There should have been a lot of blood, shouldn't there, Dr. Willis?"

"Yes."

"But I don't see any. As that neighbor said, there's hardly been any rain lately." He paused. "I may get the techs out here with luminol. See if they can find any traces of blood on the ground and the stuff around here."

Odell stopped taking photographs and said, "I've got a spray can of luminol in the cruiser's trunk, Agent Twiddy. I can get it."

Balls glanced up at the blue sky. "Too light out here now," he said. "Have to wait until almost dark or at least damn cloudy."

Odell said, "I can come back here at just before dark and use the luminol." Traces of blood, even on areas that have been scrubbed, glow blue in the dark when sprayed with luminol.

Balls just nodded, not really listening.

"I can have another deputy relieve Dorsey," Odell said.

Balls, that puzzled frown evident on his face, said, "Can't understand why we don't see some blood stains. And where's that missing shoe?"

Odell stood closer. "Not killed here?"

"I just wonder," Balls said, turning his sight around the area and off toward the woods and the faintest of a path that led out to a clearing twenty or more yards away.

Dr. Willis peeled off the latex gloves and stowed them carefully in a disposable plastic bag he retrieved from his old-fashioned oval-topped scuffed black leather medical bag. "Medics might as well take the body, if you're through now, Agent Twiddy."

Balls motioned to the medical technicians who stood silently waiting.

Duncan and the other medical technician exchanged

glances. The techs were donned in long, plastic attire that looked like HazMat suits. They had tugged on orange gloves and wore odor-filtering masks with elastic bands that hooked over their ears. They ducked under the tape, bringing with them a collapsible gurney with a neatly folded body bag atop it.

I didn't want to watch them. I turned away but remained standing there. Again I studied the clear blue sky and the tops of the pine trees there in the sun. Behind my back, I was conscious of Balls talking to Odell and Dr. Willis. ". . . not here," I heard him say. "I don't think she was killed here. She was dragged here after she was dead. Dragged from . . . somewhere." His voice trailed off.

Odell said, "By one of the bears?"

"Maybe," Balls said.

I turned and watched him.

The two medical techs stood close by. Then Duncan said, "You want us to . . . to what?"

Dr. Willis said, "She's got to go to Greenville. Autopsy. Not much I can tell about the body here. Except that she's suffered a great deal of trauma . . . several days ago."

Duncan silently nodded. The other medic looked at Duncan, a slightly sick cast to his face despite the fact that much of his face was hidden by the mask.

Dr. Willis turned to Balls, then to Odell. "The Bear Woman. What was her real name?"

Balls looked to Odell for an answer.

Odell said, "First name was Estelle. She was Estelle Byerly Sasser. Everyone just called her the Bear Woman. She'd lived out here for years, looking after bears. She was married at one time, years ago."

"Next of kin?" Balls asked.

"Not that I know of," Odell said. He shot me a meaningful glance. "She was married and divorced. Divorced from Devon Sasser, years ago."

One of the leading volunteers in the search for Odell Wright's sister that I wanted to see.

Chapter Twenty-Two

Balls pursed his lips, poking them out slightly, making that face he often did before speaking. "We'll try to notify him. Got a notify somebody. Might as well start with him." To Odell he said, "You know where he lives?"

Odell said, "I know he travels a lot. Has a traveling sales job of some sort. He used to drive a semi, long distance. That was some time back. I see him from time to time." He appeared to be contemplating Balls' question. "He lives, at least used to, in Kill Devil Hills. Bay Drive, I think."

"That's where he lives," I said. "Not far from me. I went by his house Monday to try to see him but he wasn't in."

Neither of them responded. They knew why I wanted to see him.

Instead, they watched the medics quietly push the gurney inside the vehicle, and then peel off the plastic HazMat covering and gloves, put them inside to one side, wadded up. To be disposed of, I was sure. They quietly shut the rear doors on their vehicle and went around to the front, preparing to leave.

I watched Dr. Willis trudge off to his sedan. He nodded at Deputy Dorsey as he passed. Dorsey raised a hand in what was a partial salute of some sort.

Then the three of us approached Dorsey and Odell's big vehicle. Odell opened the driver's side door and reached in for his radio. He spoke a minute or so, signed off and stepped in front of Dorsey. "I've got relief for you coming right away. Stay here until Deputy Duval gets here."

"Yes, sir," Dorsey said softly. He added, "No problem."

Odell nodded. More to himself than to Dorsey, he said, "We'll be coming back this afternoon, late." Then actually addressing Dorsey, he said, "I want the scene to stay just like it is until Agent Twiddy and I have gone over it this afternoon and evening."

Again, "Yes, sir."

Quietly, the three of us took our places in the cruiser. We moved, it seemed to me, as if enveloped in weariness. No one spoke. Before we left, however, Odell worked his fingers over the onboard computer keys. Obviously he searched some data base. He studied the screen, then turned to Balls. "Looks like Devon Sasser is still listed on Bay Drive, Kill Devil Hills.

Balls leaned forward so he could see the computer's screen. "We might as well swing by there."

I glanced at my watch. It would take us about forty minutes. The morning had slipped away.

When we got out on the highway, driving in the sunshine of that spring day, with a slip of fresh air coming in the window that Balls had lowered a couple of inches, the lethargy that had pressed upon us began to dissipate.

Balls twisted his head at me. "You still got a buy me lunch," he said. He faced forward. "After we try to give this notification." He grinned at Odell's profile. "Heck, Odell, he'll buy you lunch, too."

With the slightest trace of a smile, Odell said, "Appreciate it, but after we try to track down Devon Sasser, I'll head on back home until it's time for us to go back to the scene." Then he obviously thought of another angle. "If we can't find Sasser, there was a foundation of some sort—a group of local women who made periodic contributions to the Bear Woman. I'm sure of it. I can track them down."

We moved past an out-of-state SUV that had probably slowed a bit when the driver noticed the approaching police vehicle.

Balls said, "The Bear Woman also have money of her own or something? I had wondered how she stayed out there all those years."

"I guess she did," Odell said. "That land she was on I think came from her family, but they're all gone now, I understand."

We were silent for several miles. I saw the Virginia Dare Memorial Bridge rising up ahead of us. I decided to speak up. "After all those years of feeding the bears, and fending off hunters and others, I'm surprised the bears would attack her." I made the remark, hoping to draw Balls or Odell out a bit more concerning their theories, if they had any other than the apparent obvious—attack by a bear or bears.

But the only remark I heard came from Balls. "Those are wild animals. They ain't household pets."

Odell, his hands on the steering wheel, nodded.

I listened to the rhythmic thump-thump as we drove across the long bridge and I looked out at the water and the way the sun sparkled on it. Far in the distance a powerboat trailed a long white V-shaped wake as it moved across the sound.

After we crossed the bridge, we had to stop momentarily at the traffic light where the highways came together. Then we continued on past Pirates Cove and over the Washington Baum Bridge and Roanoke Sound. As we passed Lone Cedar and Tale of the Whale restaurants and then Sugar Creek on the left, Balls twisted back toward me and said, "Some of that shrimp at Sugar Creek. That'd be good."

"Okay," I said.

Traffic picked up on the Bypass. With Memorial Day coming up in about two more weeks, the season would get underway full steam. Already early tourists were beginning to arrive. There was a certain excitement that stirred within me at the start of the season; and at the other end of the season, there was a touch of relief that it was over, and things would get quieter and more settled. Maybe we all have these dual tugs and pulls.

As we approached the Dare Centre in Kill Devil Hills, Odell moved into the left-turn lane at Third Street. He glanced once more at his GPS and when the light changed, he drove west on Third to Bay Drive. At Bay Drive, he turned right and drove slowly. The house was on the right, with a partial view of the water across the road. The view was obstructed somewhat by a tall, narrow white house of at least three stories that perched close to the water.

Odell eased the cruiser into the driveway.

A tall, angular man was in the front yard of the house, in the process apparently of trimming lower branches of a live oak tree. He held a pair of manual clippers in his bare hands. He studied us as we stopped and Odell killed the engine. The man stood silently watching.

"That's Devon Sasser," Odell said softly.

Odell and Balls started getting out of the car. Balls tilted his head at me. "You might as well get out, too," he said, "so Sasser doesn't think you're in custody. Just hang back and keep your mouth shut."

"You know me," I said, and opened the back door.

"Yeah," Balls said.

Odell and Balls approached. Odell spoke first. "Mr. Sasser?"

Sasser stood in place, holding the clippers in his left hand. "Yep. What is it?" His gaze took in the three of us in turn. His arms were long and muscular.

Odell said, "I'm afraid, Mr. Sasser, we have some very bad news about your wife, your former wife."

Devon Sasser inclined his head toward Odell. There was a slight sagging of his shoulders. "Yes? What sort of bad news?"

Odell shifted his stance somewhat as if trying to get his feet more firmly placed. "Would you like to go inside, Mr.

Sasser?"

Sasser shook his head. "What sort of bad news?" he said again, and remained standing in place.

Odell said, "I'm afraid she's met with a very unfortunate . . . very unfortunate event." He swallowed. "She's deceased, Mr. Sasser."

Sasser leveled his eyes at Odell. "Dead?"

"Yes, sir. I'm afraid so. Hate to bring you this news, but we didn't know where else to go. Her relatives or anything."

Sasser turned his back on us and took a few halting steps over to the stairs at the side of his house. He sat heavily on one of the lower steps, staring at the ground. He jabbed the end of the clippers into the scruffy grass near his feet. The clippers stood upright. He sat there hunched over, not making eye contact with us.

Again, Odell said, "Would you like to go inside, Mr. Sasser?"

Sasser shook his head. "What happened? When? Today?"

"No, sir. We just found out about it this morning," Odell said. He took a breath. Balls hadn't said anything. He had just kept his gaze on Sasser. Odell made his voice level and even. "Apparently, Mr. Sasser, death occurred a few days ago. Maybe close to a week."

Sasser studied Odell's face, and then Balls'. He hardly looked at me. "What? What happened? She just die . . . or?"

"Examination is tentative at this time," Odell said, "but it appears she may have been attacked by a bear or bears."

"Shit," Sasser muttered. He jutted his chin out and spoke with bitterness. "Might know it. Those damn bears." He bobbed his head. "I knew it, I knew it. One of these days the bears would turn on her." He put one hand on the top of the clippers and moved them back and forth in the sod. "The Bear Woman. That's what everybody called her." He said it with a tone that was a bit derisive. "Yeah, well so much for being the Bear Woman."

For the first time, Balls spoke. "As Deputy Wright said,

attack by a bear or bears is the tentative conclusion. Her
body is being sent to Greenville for . . . for final determination." Balls took a step toward Sasser and put out his hand.
"I'm SBI Agent Twiddy. We hate to bring you this news."

Sasser glanced at Balls. Nodded his head shakily, took
Balls' hand and gave it a light shake. Sasser's body was lean,
muscular and angular but his face was round, head relatively
small, almost as if the head and body didn't match. His eyes,
behind rimless glasses, were a pale green. I had seen his picture of twenty years earlier in *The Coastland Times* articles.
Except maybe for the roundness of his face, I couldn't picture him today as the person who was a leader in the hunt for
Odell's sister. There was a mostly healed long scratch along
his left cheek, probably from the hanging limbs of the live
oak he had been trimming.

Sasser turned his attention back to Odell and addressed
him by name for the first time, although I was sure he knew
who he was. "What now, Odell? I mean me and Estelle been
divorced more'n twenty years. I mean I'm sorry she's died,
but I don't know that there's anything I can do, am supposed
to do."

Odell said, "We know you're divorced and technically
and legally there's nothing for you to do, but we wonder if
there is some next of kin, someone we need to contact."

Sasser shook his head, shoulders hunched, one hand re-
maining on the top handle of the clippers. "She didn't have
kin. They was all dead. Well, maybe there's a niece or cous-
in or something out in New Mexico or some place. But nobody close." He shook his head again. "Not a soul. Her parents been dead twenty-five or more years. They left her that
property—thirty-four acres." He made a snorting sound.
"Property was both of ours—until the divorce." Then he
looked up at Odell and Balls. "What about a funeral or burial
or something? Who pays for that?"

"We'll figure that out later," Odell said, shifting his
stance. "Meantime . . ."

Sasser interrupted. "That bunch of do-gooder women, those tree hugger types been looking after her from time to time all these years. Maybe they'll take care of it."

Odell nodded. "We'll see about that."

Balls tried for a pleasant, understanding expression on his face. He said, "When was the last time you saw her, Mr. Sasser? Saw Estelle?"

"Oh, hell, it's been quite a spell. I think the last time I saw her was back near the first of the year. I'd stopped at Stan's Market on my way back from Rocky Mount and she came in there with a wad of greasy dollar bills to buy a bunch of food and stuff. I guess for herself and those damn bears. Two or three big jars of honey and peanut butter. I remember that." He got a distressed cast to his face, then looked back up again. "I tell you the truth, I hardly recognized her. She was pretty at one time. She'd sure let herself go." He shook his head again. "Crazy. That's what she was."

There was a moment of awkward silence, shifting of feet, as if it was time to go and no one knew how to initiate the departure.

Using the handle of the clippers to leverage himself up, Sasser rose, rather shakily, glanced toward the live oak tree and then back at Odell. "You'll let me know?" He gave the tiniest shake to his head. "Whatever it is you need to let me know?"

"Yes, sir," Odell said.

Devon Sasser cast his eyes at the low branches of the life oak. "I'm tired a running into these damn branches every time I come out here." He touched the scratch on his cheek as if remembering.

As he turned away from us, I couldn't tell for sure, but there might have been the start of a tear in one of his pale eyes. Perhaps it was cynical of me, but I couldn't help but wonder if maybe that was for our benefit, because at the same time a look of some relief touched his face at our imminent departure.

Chapter Twenty-Three

We rode in silence after we left Devon Sasser. I watched Balls' profile as he stared straight ahead. We left Kill Devil Hills and entered Nags Head. Balls spoke, more to himself than to either of us: "Twenty years divorced."

Odell glanced over at Balls and then back at the road. He seemed to have read Balls' unspoken thoughts. "Yes, sir. I guess I don't expect he'd have much emotion left for her."

Balls nodded.

I didn't know but what Devon Sasser was showing as much emotion as he ever showed. He certainly took the news of his ex-wife's death stoically. Except maybe right there at the end it might have gotten to him a little. Hard to tell, and I tried to curb the bit of cynicism that I felt.

We stopped for one of the traffic lights at Tanger Outlet Mall. Odell said, "You want me to take you to your car? Or just drop you off at Sugar Creek and come back pick you up later this afternoon?"

Balls shifted in his seat. "Oh, might as well just drop us off." He tossed his head toward me. "That fellow in the backseat's going to buy me lunch. Come back and pick us up, say, about three-thirty?" Again referring to me, Balls said, "Knowing him, he'll most likely wanna go with us this afternoon."

Odell pulled into the parking area of Sugar Creek. "See

you at three-thirty," Odell said.

As we went up the steps and inside, owner Irvin Bateman stood in front of the hostess's desk talking with an older woman behind the desk. He smiled at us and we shook hands. The woman turned to a younger woman, said something, and gave her two menus, and we followed the younger woman to the left and around the bar. She wore shorts and a Sugar Creek T-shirt. She seated us at a table overlooking the water. It was a pretty view. She said Jenny or Jean would look after us. We thanked her and she left and I watched her walk away.

Balls leaned toward me. "Couldn't help but eye her, could you?"

"Just being polite," I said.

"Uh-huh."

When Jenny or Jean came to the table we ordered the special of twenty fried shrimp. Jenny or Jean was younger than the other woman who had shown us to our table. She also wore shorts. In just a few minutes she brought our food. "Enjoy," she said.

"Keep your eyes on the food," Balls mumbled to me as she left.

The shrimp were lightly breaded and smelled good. I'd opted for a baked potato rather than French fries; we both had cucumber salads and cornbread that had a hint of sweetness in it. I went to work on my baked potato, lavishing it with butter, sour cream, and then a bit of pepper and a dash of salt. Balls studied my potato. Then deftly he reached over with his fork and dug out a good size bite of the potato, making sure to get a glob of half-melted butter and sour cream. He chewed appreciatively. "Good," he said. "Maybe I should have ordered a baked potato."

I extended my hand and clipped one of his fries, plopped it in my mouth. "Your fries are good," I said.

We ate mostly in silence. I wasn't sure whether I'd be able to finish all of my shrimp. They were fat and succulent.

You didn't have to scrape off any of the breading, it was so light. I wasn't sure I could keep out of my mind what we had seen earlier that day. But I did and every now and then I'd look out the wide windows to the water of Sugar Creek and Ballast Point and toward Shallow Bag Bay beyond. The view was hard to beat.

During a pause in the meal, just to make conversation, I asked Balls, "How's Lorraine?"

He didn't answer right away. He toyed with a shrimp, pushing it around with his fork, and stared at his plate. Then he looked up at me. "Tell you the truth, Weav, she's not doing all that great. Now that both kids are out on their own, I don't know, she seems sort of lost or something." He gave a slight shrug. "Worries about her health and stuff. She used to never mention health. Now she talks about different ailments she's afraid she may have."

"Sorry to hear that," I said, my voice soft.

"I'm trying to get her to go to the doctor, get a checkup. But she doesn't want to." Then he tried a grin. "Hell, she doesn't even bitch anymore about my being gone so much of the time, working."

I tried a bit of levity also. "Probably glad to get you out of her hair."

"Yeah, maybe so," he said. But there was no joy in his tone. Then he frowned at what was left of my baked potato. "You eat the skin and all?"

I cut a bite. "Yes. It's excellent. Good vitamins and stuff in the skin."

He nodded but wasn't really thinking about my potato. He got back to Lorraine, and he gave me one of his big grins. "The only time she really perks up is when she says something about how she'd like to go back to Paris."

"Hell," I said, "let's plan it. In the fall? I think that'd be great. I know Elly would love to go back."

"Yeah," he said, "and we can be chaperones again. Keep you from violating that lovely young woman." His grin was back full blast and I was glad.

"We'll do it," I said.

We finished off the meal with coffee and then went out-side to stroll along the dock, sit out on the gazebo in the sun and look at the water and the blue sky. From time to time, Balls checked his watch. After a while he said that we'd best go around front and wait for Odell. It was almost time.

Right at three-thirty Odell pulled up and we got in the cruiser.

To Odell, Balls said, "You see your family? Get to spend a little time?"

"Yes, sir. It was nice. Both the kids wanted me to stay, but I told them I'd be back by suppertime." He pulled out on the highway and glanced over at Balls. "I think we will be back by then? Six o'clock or so?"

"Should be," Balls said.

When we pulled into the area with the yellow crime scene tape, Deputy Duval stood near the tape talking with three men. One of them I recognized as Wyatt Wilkinson from this morning. The other two, roughly half Wilkinson's age, were dressed similarly in jeans and work shirts. I figured they were probably more of his neighbors.

Odell approached Deputy Duval, who came forward to meet him. The three others hung back and watched us. Duval was one of the older deputies, almost as old as Odell. He had dark brown hair that he parted and brushed to one side and he wore cop sunglasses so it was hard to see his eyes. He looked fit and he held his stomach in, head erect.

"Who're they?" Odell said. "We met Wilkinson this morning."

Duval jerked a thumb back to the right behind the trailer. "They live back over that way. The other two are brothers or cousins or something. Got the same last names. Cummins. Jeff and Robert Cummins."

Odell nodded. "Keep them out of the way."

"Will do," Duval said.

Balls took a few steps toward the three men. "Where'd she feed the bears?"

Wilkinson pointed to the faint path off to the left. "Down that way," he said. "Get past these trees and stuff and it opens up like a field."

The Cummins duo mumbled agreement with Wilkinson. "I'd seen her down there—from a distance." He gave a chuckle and shook his head. "Damn sure didn't want a get too close." As if remembering, he wrinkled his brow and said, "One or two of them black bears'd come right out of the woods and up to her. There was a big ol' male bear that I think was her favorite."

Balls said, "Thanks," and he turned to Odell. "Let's take a walk down that way."

I wormed my way closer to Balls and Odell as if it were only natural that I tag along. Balls didn't pay any attention to me. He and Odell walked side-by-side. I followed. Duval stayed in place and made sure the three neighbors did the same.

The sun was getting lower but it was still warm and I could smell the pine trees and the heat coming off the tall underbrush that grew on each side of the faint path. We walked slowly. Balls and Odell studied the ground intently. After several yards, I glanced back over my shoulder. The trailer and yellow tape were no longer visible.

Then we saw the woman's missing sneaker at the edge of the path. We left it there, undisturbed.

Another twenty yards or so and suddenly the path opened onto an almost circular clearing of at least thirty or more feet across. Beyond the circular clearing, with a short pathway leading to it, a meadow of two or three acres lay ahead. I concentrated on the large field, maybe half expecting to see a black bear lumber out on the clearing like I had seen last week when I visited the Bear Woman. I wasn't paying attention to Balls and Odell, but Balls had bent down low and stared at the ground. "Bingo," he said.

I turned to look where he was pointing. Brownish stains were splattered on the scrub grass, bits of old leaves, and bare dirt.

Odell looked solemn. "Yes sir, this is where it happened."

Balls continued to study the ground. He took in the area with a slow sweep of his eyes. "We'll collect a sample to make sure it's hers. But no doubt about it." He gave a rueful shake of his head. "Don't need luminol to know that's blood." He turned to me as if he suddenly realized I was there. "How about you running back to the cruiser and get the camera again."

"Sure," I said, and hurried away the same way we had come, careful not to scuff up the path. When I returned with the Canon, I took several shots, some focusing up close, others back a few steps to give perspective. I offered the camera to Odell, but he shook his head and said, "I think you've got it documented, except for that sneaker. Don't mind, step back and get a picture of it."

Odell pulled a clear plastic bag from his windbreaker jacket and carefully lifted a stained leaf and dropped it into the bag. Then three more leaves.

Balls peered at the ground behind us, up to the path we had used. "The blood is here and doesn't appear to go anywhere else." He was quiet a moment, a frown on his face. As if talking to himself, he said, "She bled out here. Plenty of it here. Bled out completely. Dead. Right here." He looked back toward the way we had come. "Then how in hell she get back up to the trailer?"

Odell had gone to the left edge of the circular clearing. "Here's something else, Agent Twiddy, that's sort of puzzling."

Balls stepped carefully over to where Odell stood.

Odell pointed to the ground. "Somebody started digging

here. The diggings don't look old, either."

The shovel marks, several of them close together, were four or five inches deep, and they did, indeed, look as though they had been made recently.

Odell rubbed his chin. "Maybe she'd started digging when the bear or bears attacked her. Whoever started digging didn't finish."

It was quiet. I didn't even hear any birds.

"Yeah," Balls said, casting his eyes about, "but where in hell is the shovel?"

Chapter Twenty-Four

I remembered the short-handled shovel the Bear Woman had with her when she tended that little garden. I'd take a look back there but didn't think I'd find it.

We walked the path toward the trailer slowly and carefully, studying the path once again as we proceeded. Balls said, "Too light to use the luminol, but I don't think we really need it." He kept his head down, peering at the ground as he talked. "She bled out back in that clearing. Don't think we're going to find any traces of blood up this way." He shook his head. More to himself he muttered, "How she ended up back at the trailer . . . that's a puzzler."

When we got within sight of the circle of crime scene tape, Balls and Odell stopped to confer. I hung back a step or so. Balls turned to Odell. "It still looks like she was attacked by a bear or bears, as we all assume. If so, and if that's confirmed, I don't have any more business here. But we'll wait on officially getting it ruled as a bear attack until we get the autopsy."

Odell nodded his head solemnly, looking serious, no smile.

Balls continued, his voice low as if conferring with himself. "But a couple of things don't fit . . ." His voice trailed off. "Want to get the autopsy report. Be a couple of days or so." Glancing at the trailer, he said aloud, "Meantime, we got

a keep this area secure. Keep those good ol' boys from mes-
sing with things."

"Agreed," Odell said. "Not sure the sheriff will okay
keeping a deputy out here all night, but we can secure the
scene, warn those guys there, put the fear of God in 'em, and
see if we can't lock up the trailer. I'm sure we can get someone out here in the morning."

"That should do it," Balls said. He puffed out a breath of
air, thinking. "And as far as we know, this is not an actual
crime scene." He managed a halfway grin. "Not like we can
charge those bears."

We approached Deputy Duval and the three men, who
stood there, feet shuffling, eyeing us. Odell spoke softly to
Duval and then Odell ducked under the tape and went to the
door of the trailer. He took a deep breath and stepped inside.
He came back out in less than a minute. He held up a key
that must have been hanging just inside the door. Locking
the door and trying it to make sure, he held up a victory
thumb, and slipped the key into his pocket.

Odell came back to Duval and the trio. Balls walked
over to stand beside Odell and stare hard at the men. "Okay,
gentlemen," Odell said, addressing the three men, "we'd like
for you to leave the site now. This is a crime scene area and
we've got to keep it completely clear until we finish this investigation." He looked steadily at the men, one after the
other. "Time to go back to your residences."

Wyatt Wilkinson and the others gave little shrugs. With
a quick smile, Wilkinson said, "Okay." They began to shuf-
fle away, talking among themselves.

"Hang here for about thirty more minutes, Duval, then
you can take off," Odell said. "We'll get someone else out
here in the morning, or I'll come out, make sure everything
is still okay."

We were well out on the highway before anyone spoke.
Balls checked his watch, then to Odell he said, "You're gonna be able get home in plenty of time before supper, see the

kiddies."

With a nod, Odell said, "Good."

"And I'll pick up my car at the courthouse, head home myself. Get back to Elizabeth City area in time for a fashionably late supper." He inclined his head toward the backseat. "Just have to drop off this dirty-neck newspaper guy at his house."

Odell grinned and kept his eyes straight ahead on the highway.

Balls drove on to my house and I told him I hoped Lorraine got to feeling better. He thanked me and said, "Me too."

Inside, I spoke to Janey and checked her food supply and water. Gave her another small sprig of millet seed and fresh water. Spoiling her. She bobbed her head in appreciation. I had intended to leave the radio on for her; she enjoys the noise. But I'd forgotten to do it.

So I turned the television on to one of the news channels. Then I thought about what I needed to eat for dinner. But then . . . Oh, my God. I'd planned to go to the movie with Elly. With everything going on, I'd completely forgotten it. Glanced at the time. Getting close to six.

I called Elly. The phone rang at least three full times before she answered.

"I just came in from outside," she said, sounding a little breathless but cheerful. "And what have you been up to today?"

"The Pioneer Theater," I said. "We were supposed to go to the movie tonight, but—"

"Oh, Harrison," she said. "I forgot all about it. I'm so sorry . . ."

"Actually, I forgot about it, too, Elly." I took a breath. "There's been a lot going on today . . ." I knew that tomorrow when she got to the courthouse—if not before then—she'd hear all about the Bear Woman. So I told her everything, start to finish.

She was quiet for a moment or two. Then she said, "I can't believe the bears killed her. They loved her. She fed them for years."

"I know," I said.

"Linda did a feature story on her a couple of years ago. She was impressed with how friendly the bears were with her. Linda had to stay back quite a ways but she watched the woman feed one of the bears."

Linda Shackleford, a long-time friend of Elly's, was a reporter and photographer with *The Coastland Times*. I knew she'd be on the story, along with other reporters, by first thing in the morning. Frankly, I was a little surprised we hadn't seen any reporters out at the site today. Don't guess the word had filtered out yet, but most of them had police scanners and could have heard about it that way.

Elly continued her musings. "I know several of the women who formed that, whatever you call it, to raise money from time to time to help the Bear Woman buy food—for herself and for the bears."

I heard commotion in the background, and Mrs. Pedersen saying something to Martin, who sounded like he was crying or at least fussing.

"Just a minute, Martin," Elly called. Back to me, she said, "Harrison, I'm going to have to tend to Martin. He's cross and fussy and it's not even bedtime yet."

"I understand," I said. Then, "Sorry about the movie. How about lunch tomorrow? Let me take you to lunch. Noon?"

"Sounds lovely. I'm sorry about the movie, too. But we'll do it soon."

For dinner, I settled for what is usually a typical Sunday night supper: a bowl of cereal, and two leftover biscuits split open and adorned with Fontina cheese, which went in the toaster oven, and two small patties of precooked sausage. When it was prepared, I took it to the coffee table and ate while watching the news.

I figured that a little after eight o'clock I would call Elly

again. I wasn't exactly at what we call loose ends, but I kept
mulling over in my mind the events of the day. I couldn't get
over the fact that the Bear Woman was killed in the little
clearing but her body, what was left of it, ended up back at
her trailer, practically at the doorsteps. Too, the digging
marks from a shovel near where she was killed—but no
shovel. All indications were that she was attacked by a bear
or bears, the ones she had befriended. But just the same . . .

I tried to think of something else. When I finished with
my cereal, sausage and toasted cheese biscuits, and rinsed
the bowl and spoon, cleaned up the kitchen a bit, I decided to
at least play a few riffs on the bass. Playing would help to
keep my fingers limbered up and toughened, plus maybe get
my mind off the Bear Woman. I muted the television and
took the bass from its stand. Janey liked hearing me play,
too, not that she had any appreciation of music, but she certainly liked the noise and activity.

Despite playing the bass and trying not to think about
the Bear Woman or Odell's long-missing sister, my mind
kept flipping back to one or the other. I played maybe seven
or eight minutes—including the melody line of "As Time
Goes By"—and laid the bass down on its side there in the
middle of the living room floor, as per usual.

Janey chirped and said, "Shit." She wanted me to continue playing, creating sound and activity.

Taking my seat in the little chair by the phone, I checked
the time. I would call Elly in a few minutes. But right then I
was frankly feeling—what?—a little guilt that I wasn't making any real progress in uncovering the slightest lead on
Odell's missing sister. I sighed and picked up the phone and
called Elly. She answered on the beginning of the second
ring.

We didn't talk long. Just more or less to touch base with
each other and say good night and sweet dreams.

I got out of the chair and walked toward the kitchen,
passing Janey's cage on the way. She eyed me and said,

"Bitch," the other word in her vocabulary.

"Who you talking about, Janey?"

She chirped and did her jerky head-bobbing dance.

By eleven-thirty the next morning, I was well on my way to Manteo. I parked across the street from the courthouse. I had time to duck into Downtown Books and speak to owner Jamie and see what was going on. She's a favorite and always supportive of writers. She had ordered for me a copy of *Hemingway in Love*, a memoir by Hemingway's friend of many years, A. E. Hotchner. I paid for the slim book and tucked it under my arm and went up a couple of doors to the old brick courthouse.

In the Register of Deeds office, Janet saw me approach the counter and she called back to Elly, who was in the small office off the main section, "There's someone special here to see you, Elly." Her voice was that usual teasing singsong.

Elly came out, a nice smile on her face. She wore a peach colored cotton blouse and the off-white, tailored slacks that showed off her trim hips and bottom so nicely. Her hair was pinned up and I loved looking at her porcelain-white neck. She had lived here at the Outer Banks all of her life and yet her skin remained untouched by the sun, it seemed. She came around the counter, still smiling, and stood close to me.

"Ready for lunch?" I said.

"Absolutely."

I leaned in to catch her scent, that faint aroma of a very light cologne and sun-freshened cotton. She gave me an impish smile and tucked her hand into the crook of my arm.

We walked down Sir Walter Raleigh Street past Downtown Books and Jeremy Blevins' place to Ortega'z. We were seated in a booth and both of us ordered the grilled chicken tacos from a friendly young man who said his name was Terry. The taco salads arrived in their freshly made spinach tortilla bowls and were very tasty, with small containers of salsa and sour cream on the side.

Naturally we talked about the Bear Woman and I asked Elly if she was hearing anything new there in the courthouse, where the word spread with warp speed. She said she had talked with Mabel, a fount of information, but not much beyond what I had told her on the phone last night.

"I do know," she said, "that they are trying to find if there are any relatives at all. There's that ex-husband of course, but apparently he hasn't had anything to do with her in years. So far, they haven't found anyone. Any relatives."

"Why'd they get divorced? You know?" I figured it had something to do with the affair Harvey Mitchell had been having with her, but I didn't say anything about that.

"No," Elly said. "Mabel did say they'd been divorced twenty years or more."

Elly eyed me. "What are you thinking?"

"Oh, nothing," I said.

She gave me one of her raised eyebrow looks. "You're never thinking 'oh, nothing,' Mr. Crime Writer. I know you."

I grinned. "Just thinking how good this taco salad is."

"Um-huh."

After we'd finished eating, we strolled back toward the courthouse, her shoulder touching my upper arm lightly from time to time. When we got to the steps of the courthouse, Elly said, "Thanks again for the lunch." She glanced around, then said, "Any great insight into the disappearance of Deputy Odell Wright's sister?"

I shook my head. "Nothing. Nada. I just hope I haven't increased more anxiety or expectation in Odell's mind by just reading the old files and talking to some people."

"Who knows, Mr. Crime Writer. If anyone can come up with leads, I'd bet on you."

"Thanks for the vote of confidence. But honestly I don't see anything other than a dead end."

She gave a slight shrug and smiled. "Again, who knows? Just maybe . . ."

Chapter Twenty-Five

Saturday morning, I waked by seven and shuffled into the kitchen to fix coffee, uncovering Janey's cage as I slouched past her. The French Roast coffee smelled good and I felt more alert even before it was ready. Taking my coffee, I started toward the sliding door to the deck. The sun was bright and cheery, promising another beautiful day in May.

As I passed the mirror on the wall near the sliding door, I frowned at my image, shook my head. My eyes were puffy and red; my hair looked like rabbits had been playing in it and my face like a crumpled-up newspaper. "My lord," I muttered. Glad no one could see me. Elly said I was handsome. Good thing she wasn't looking at me now.

Standing out on the deck, drinking the fresh, strong black coffee, and breathing in the fine ocean air, I began to feel more alive. I believed I could actually feel my face uncrumpling. A soft breeze made my hair wiggle. I tried patting it down in the back with the palm of my free hand. Needed a haircut. Oh, well. The tortured poet look.

Taking a seat on one of the Kmart webbed chairs I used on the deck, I placed my coffee mug on the little wrought-iron table to my right. I'd just taken another sip of coffee when the phone rang. I'm sure I frowned again, checking my watch. It was only just past seven-thirty.

I went inside. The phone's ID screen displayed Balls'

cell phone number. I picked up just as the third ring started.

I mumbled something as a sort of hello.

Balls started right in: "Time you were up and about anyway. Especially if you're buying me a three-egg omelet with ham and cheese at Henry's."

I knew there had to be something up or Balls wouldn't be coming down here again so early in the morning. "Okay, Balls," I said, "tell me what brings you here."

"You gonna buy me breakfast or not?"

"Food in exchange for information. Right?"

"Right." Then there was the slightest pause and I could sense he shifted from his usual banter to something much more serious.

I heard him take a breath. "We got a homicide."

I exclaimed, "What . . . who?"

"The Bear Woman. No doubt about it."

"Jeeze." But I'll admit I wasn't totally surprised. "Autopsy?"

"Autopsy was called in last evening to Sheriff Albright. Much quicker than I thought it would be." I could hear road noise. "I'll be at Henry's in thirty minutes. You meeting me there? Buy me one of those three-egg omelets? Ham and cheese. Maybe mushrooms too. Even with lump crabmeat."

"Hearty appetite. Okay. Tell me details then?"

"Sure," he said. It was impossible to tell whether he meant it or was just blowing me off.

"Thirty minutes," I said. "See you there."

I showered, threw on some clothes—khaki slacks, golf shirt, and planned to grab my windbreaker on the way out. Tried to tame my hair a little and then gave up. Shortly after eight I parked there at Henry's. The lot was always crowded at breakfast.

I went inside. "There'll be two of us," I told the young hostess. She led me to the third booth back on the left. Less than five minutes later I saw Balls back his Thunderbird into a space near the entrance. He came in wearing his tan cotton sports jacket. His presence dwarfed the tiny hostess who led him back to my booth. As he slid into the booth, I glimpsed the empty holster strapped to his belt. His wicked .45 caliber Glock was undoubtedly stowed under the front seat of his locked car. He was ready for business.

But first he had to be Balls. He frowned at me. "When you getting a haircut?" he said.

"Good to see you too, Balls."

"You ordered yet?"

"Waiting for you. Figured you'd show up after a while."

The waitress came to our booth, her order pad in hand. She appeared to be in her late thirties and was all business. She started by rote reciting today's omelet specials and Balls interrupted her.

"I want a three-egg omelet with ham and American cheese, mushrooms, and some black olives if you got 'em and maybe some lump crab meat, too," Balls said and grinned.

She looked at him as if he might request something additional. Then she said, "Biscuits or toast?"

"Toast. White bread. Make it an extra order of toast."

She nodded, and scribbled on her order pad. "Hash browns or grits?"

"Hash browns," Balls said. "Oh, jelly, too."

"Jelly's right there," she said, flicking her hand at the container on our table that held an assortment of jellies. "Extra butter, too." She turned a tired smile on me.

"Ham and American cheese omelet," I said. "Hash browns and whole wheat toast. Thank you."

"Drinks? Besides water?"

"Coffee for me," Balls said.

"Tomato juice, please, with ice."

She left us and Balls said, "Tomato juice? You got a hangover?"

"Not for many years," I said. With an open hand, I waved away any further banter. "Okay, Balls, let's get to it. Tell me what's up."

He nodded. Serious again. "Dr. Mordecai faxed in the autopsy report last evening to Sheriff Albright. Sheriff also called her and talked a bit. It seems that wound on the back of her skull wasn't a powerful bite by a bear. She was struck in the head with a fairly sharp object. Something like maybe an ax."

I waited a moment or two. "Or the edge of a shovel," I said.

He got a sly grin. "Yeah, maybe that *missing* shovel."

I said, "That's what killed her? The blow to the head?"

"Yeah."

"Not the bears, after all."

He nodded an affirmative. We were both quiet for a minute or more, lost in our own thoughts. Then Balls said, "You know that massive looking wound on her left shoulder . . ."

"I tried not to look at her—what was left of her—that much, Balls. But, yes, I saw it."

"Well, there was like a big bite mark on her left shoulder. But the interesting thing, Dr. Mordecai said, that bite mark—or bite marks—was caused postmortem, after she was already dead."

The waitress came with our food.

"That was quick," Balls said.

With a lifting of the right corner of her lip, she managed a tiny smile at Balls. "It took just a little longer with your order," she said, "while the cooks hunted up all the ingredients."

"You're a sweetheart," Balls said.

She looked right friendly as she said, "Enjoy," and left.

Balls glanced quickly at me before turning his attention to his food. "But here's the curious thing . . ." He dug into his omelet, slathering two halves of his buttered toast with at least three small packets of jelly, "Dr. Mordecai said the left shoulder looked more like a bear had clamped onto it to drag her . . . not bite her."

"That's really weird, Balls." I took a big sip of my tall

tomato juice. There was crushed ice in it and it tasted great.

With his mouth full, Balls mumbled, "Yeah, it's weird all right. But what's even weirder to think about is that somebody—or some *thing*—dragged her from where she was killed to practically the front steps of her trailer."

I stopped eating. Stared at him. "You think one of her bears—what? Carried her . . . carried her home?"

He shrugged. "I don't know. It's a strange world we live in, Weav."

I thought about it. Shook my head, but not necessarily in disbelief; more in agreement that it is, indeed, a strange world we live in.

We ate in silence for a few minutes. Then I said, "So what's next?"

He swallowed, took a sip of his coffee. The waitress came back and poured fresh coffee in his mug. "Thanks," he said. She nodded, and even smiled. Holding his upright fork in one hand and the knife in the other, he looked over at me. "What I'm gonna do is go back out there and have a little talk with those good ol' boys, the ones we've already seen. Maybe some of those good ol' boys ain't as good as they seem." He chuckled, food still in his mouth. "Sort of kill two birds with one stone, so to speak. I got a talk to those two younger ones anyway. Pretty sure they're the ones mixed up in a little drug business over at their place."

I ignored the drug part, and went back to who may have killed the Bear Woman. "She was said to have been pretty tough on some of the neighbors, hunters, and others out there," I said.

"Yeah, she weren't too damn popular," he said. "Maybe one of 'em had had enough of her."

I had almost finished my omelet. "You going to be talking to some of them today?"

"You paying for this meal?"

"Yes." Then I said, "I want to see that."

"What?"

"The interviews you're thinking about."

He appeared to be thinking about it. He held one of the triangles of toast in his hand. The toast was rich with butter and grape jelly. He folded the toast into a fatter triangle and poked it into his mouth. "Okay," he said, talking over the toast, "but keep out of the way and keep your mouth shut."

"Agreed," I said. I knew I was lucky that he'd let me tag along. But he knew I'd stay out of the way, keep my mouth shut, and not write anything at all until it was clear to do so. At the same time, I was thinking that I needed to call Rose, my editor, because this was developing into one hell of a story.

Outside, we stood by the locked Thunderbird while he pulled his cell phone from his belt. "Calling Odell," he said.

I stepped a few paces toward my car.

When he finished his short call, he unlocked his car. Before he got in, he said, "Odell is having Deputy Duval stir up those good citizens from yesterday. That Wilkinson guy and those two cousins or whatever they were."

"Duval out at the site?"

"He or someone's been there since the sheriff got that call about the autopsy. An actual crime scene now. A homicide crime scene."

Balls followed me the short distance south to my house where I left my car and got in his Thunderbird.

As we headed to Manteo, I couldn't help but wonder whether there'd be more likelihood of solving this one than there was with the sad mystery of Odell's little sister. At least this was current. A better chance.

Chapter Twenty-Six

At the courthouse, we transferred once again into Odell's vehicle. He looked tired. A brushing of silvery whiskers was visible against his coffee-colored skin. Maybe a half-day's growth, like he hadn't had time to shave this morning. Both of his hands gripped the steering wheel and he stared straight ahead.

"You on duty again last night?" Balls asked, glancing over at Odell.

"After the sheriff got the autopsy report, I came out and stayed until eleven when Dorsey came on. Then Duval at seven this morning." He gave a short chuckle. "Duval said that Dorsey swore to him that about dawn he saw one of those black bears peeping out of the woods at him." With something of a grin still on his face, Odell shook his head. Then, "Oh, Duval said the Wilkinson fellow, the one who called it in, and those two Cummins buddies of his, came around about thirty minutes ago. I told him to keep them there."

"Good," Balls said. "Want to have a little sit down with those good citizens."

Odell nodded. "Figured," he said. "Oh, and Sheriff Albright made it official that he's requesting your assistance on this."

Balls nodded. "Good. For the record."

In about fifteen minutes of driving, we navigated the tiny road into the Bear Woman's compound. It was beginning to look familiar to me. We stopped near the trailer. The crime scene tape sagged a bit from the overnight dew.

Before we had gotten out of the vehicle Balls said, "We need to get some scene tape around that little clearing where we know she was actually killed."

Odell eased out of the driver's seat. "I did that last night," he said.

Balls nodded at him, an expression on his face that I recognized as approval and complimentary. "Good for you," he said. "Might have known you'd take care of it."

The three of us approached Deputy Duval. Even though the sun was out, it was mostly shady there at the trailer, but Duval still wore those cop sunglasses. Wyatt Wilkinson and the two Cummins stood back a few paces and eyed us steadily. Then Wilkinson shuffled his feet and gave a quick grin and a bob of his head.

Duval addressed Odell. "I've told them to stay here, like you said. That you and Agent Twiddy would like to talk to them."

"Good, but first we want to take another look at the clearing up there where . . . where she died," Balls said.

"Sir?" It was Wilkinson. He had taken a step forward.

Balls turned back to face him. "Yeah? What is it?"

"Sir, I don't know much about this sort of thing," Wilkinson said, his Adam's apple moving up and down on his scrawny neck, "but seems to me there's a whole lot of police activity if she was killed by one of those bears. Me and the Cummins here can't help but been wondering . . ."

Balls looked steadily at him. "We have to make sure that's what happened."

Wilkinson appeared prepared to say something else. Instead he just mumbled, "Yessir."

To Duval, Balls said, "Keep them here."

Balls, Odell and I walked along the edge of the path that

led to the clearing. Balls and Odell studied the path carefully as we went. We also looked to each side. At one point, Balls stopped and bent over to examine the path. "Looks like these are marks where she could have been dragged toward the trailer." He shook his head. "Been too long to really tell." He straightened up and we moved slowly up to the clearing.

We stood at the edge of the clearing and Balls slowly swept the area once again with his eyes. Odell did the same. Balls shook his head. "Not much here to tell us anything. A patch of blood that we already know about. Those digs over there by a shovel. Someone starting to dig, maybe . . ."

I didn't think it would hurt if I spoke up. "Maybe she had started to dig when someone came up behind her."

Balls gave me something of a look. "We can speculate all we want to but we don't know, one, whether she was digging, or two, whether someone else was digging, or three, even when these few shovel marks were made . . . and whether they have a damn thing to do with anything."

"Agreed," Odell said.

Okay, I'd had a bit of a comment and had it promptly shot down. I'd continue to keep quiet.

Balls turned to Odell. "Let's go back to the trailer. I want to talk to Mr. Tall- Lean-and-Lanky."

"Wilkinson?"

"Yeah. You keep the Cummins cousins back so I can speak to Wilkinson without them hearing. Then I'll talk individually with each of them." He cast his eyes at the ground, shook his head again, and I thought he might actually spit in disgust. "Trying to get a handle on this—almost a week after she's killed—and we've just got these good ol' boys . . ." His voice trailed off. "Ain't a helluva lot to go on for starters." Then, however, he took a deep breath, straightened his stance, and said, "But we've unraveled some that looked hopeless in the beginning. Can't let myself get discouraged before we even start." The last statement was obviously directed more at himself than at either Odell or me.

When we walked back to the trailer, Odell told Wilkinson that Agent Twiddy wanted to talk with him. Odell kept the Cummins back several yards. Balls went over to the two steps attached to the trailer. He sat down and Odell brought Wilkinson over to stand in front of Balls. Balls looked up at Odell. "Chief Deputy Wright, please make sure you get Mr. Wilkinson's full name and address. How we can get back with him."

I stood back near the side of the trailer, trying to appear invisible, yet close enough to hear what was being said.

Balls turned his gaze on Wilkinson but didn't say a word for close to a minute. Wilkinson shuffled his feet, flexed his shoulders and neck, and looked around, anywhere but at Balls who continued to stare at him. "Other than the other morning when you came upon her body, when was the last time you saw the deceased?"

"Oh, I don't know. I seen her from time to time, especially out there in the pasture." Wilkinson licked his lips. "See, I live just over yonder, next little road off the highway. I can practically see her pasture from my front yard." He gave a short laugh. "I've seen her feeding those bears . . . but from a real smart distance."

"I'll ask you again. When was the last time you remember seeing her alive?"

"I'm not trying to not answer you. I just don't know for sure. Maybe two weeks, maybe three. Last time I saw her she wasn't feeding the bears but was just sort of walking out there in her pasture, and then she turned and started walking back this way, toward this trailer."

"You spend much time watching her?"

"Oh, no sir. I ain't no Peeping Tom or nothing like that. But I do keep my eyes peeled about what goes on around here."

"Did you see people coming to visit her? Can you see her road from your place?"

"I can see the first part of her road. The beginning of it

mostly." He stretched his neck again. "Ever once in a great while I'd see that van the women drive who bring her food and money and stuff. Those women in Manteo, I guess."

"How'd you know what they were doing?"

"Oh, ever'body knows that."

Balls nodded. "You see anybody else come up?"

"Well, once in a great while."

"When was the last time?"

"Just last week. One day this little station wagon eased on to the road real slow. Then the next day, maybe the day after, this big fancy Jeep-thing drove in. Didn't pay any attention to when either one of them left."

I figured the "little station wagon" was my Outback.

Wilkinson put his hands in his pockets and leaned slightly forward toward Balls. There was a touch of aggression in his stance. "Now, I don't mean to be, you know, sort of coming at you, Mister . . ."

"Agent Twiddy."

"I don't mean to be coming across like, you know, like I'm not wanting to talk, Agent Twiddy, but it seems to me like you're thinking something besides bears. Like maybe something else happened to her. Otherwise, I don't know why you'd be asking me all these questions."

Balls pursed his lips, staring at Wilkinson, obviously thinking how to respond. "Tell you the truth, Mr. Wilkinson, there's strong indication that she wasn't killed by bears, that a human person killed her."

Wilkinson narrowed his eyes. His jaw muscles flexed. He took his hands out of his pocket and placed them on his thighs, flexing his fingers. "Now let me tell you something, Mister . . . Agent Twiddy. If you're thinking I had anything to do with that woman's killing, well, you got another thought coming. I'll tell you that. Right in a damn minute." His voice had risen in pitch as he talked. With the back of one sleeve, he wiped at his mouth, and stood straight, his shoulders back, as much as they would go.

Balls didn't appear at all fazed by Wilkinson's rather emotional outburst. "No, Mr. Wilkinson. I'm not indicating that I think you necessarily had anything to do with her death. But we're trying to fit together all the pieces of this puzzle. Find out what everybody knows. And there're lots of things that are puzzling. Like we think she was killed down there in that little clearing. Yet her body ends up here by the trailer. How'd that happen?"

Wilkinson twisted his head and shoulders in what could be interpreted as a shrug. "I don't know. If that's where she was killed at and then ended up here, my guess would be those damn bears drugged her up here—after they done killed her."

Balls nodded. "Thank you, Mr. Wilkinson. We'll be back with you if we need to talk more. But I appreciate your talking with me and giving me your views."

"Yeah. Okay," Wilkinson mumbled. He appeared he wasn't sure what to do next. He said, "I reckon I'd better get on back over to my place."

"Just give your address and phone number to Chief Deputy Wright," Balls said.

"I already done that."

As Wilkinson left, Balls rose from the steps, stretched his back, and said to Odell, "Bring the Cummins boys over, one at a time." Balls remained standing near the trailer door. "No, bring 'em both at the same time. Be okay."

The two Cummins came near the steps of the trailer. Balls continued standing. "You boys wanna sit?" Balls flipped a hand toward the steps.

"We're fine," one of them said.

"Okay. I been sitting enough myself. Now, tell me again what your names are. I know your last name's Cummins."

The slightly taller one said, "I'm Jeff." He gave a quick tilt to his head. "This is Robert." They both appeared to be in their mid- to late-thirties, maybe forty. Jeff maybe a year or two older than Robert. Their hair was dark brown, almost black, and long. Heavy eyebrows. Neither had shaved for several days. Their jeans and sweatshirts were dirty, greasy looking.

"You boys brothers, cousins?"

Jeff Cummins said, "We're half-brothers. Same mama, different daddies." He got a slight smile, maybe a little embarrassed, like he wanted to explain. "Our mama was a Cummins."

Balls nodded.

For the first time, Robert spoke. "Jeff's near 'bout two years older'n me."

Balls looked from one to the other. "What sort of work you two do?"

Jeff said, "Some fishing out of Wanchese when they're busy, the fish running."

"And some construction," Robert said. "We're real good at framing. Not many people good at that."

Balls studied his hands a moment. "You boys do any hunting."

"Oh, yeah," Robert said. "Lotta deer, rabbits, squirrels in these woods."

Jeff leaned slightly toward Balls. "But we don't shoot no bears."

Robert got a grin on his face. "When that Bear Woman'd yell at us, we'd yell back at her that we won't shooting her damn bears." He shook his head, the grin beginning to fade. "She tell us get off her property or she'd sic them bears at us."

Balls studied Robert's face. "You have a lot of arguments with that woman? Because to tell you the truth, Jeff, there's strong evidence that maybe the bears didn't kill her. That something else, or someone, killed her."

Robert knitted his brow, a look of incredulity spreading over his face. "No shit."

Jeff folded his arms across his chest. He scowled at Balls. "Just a minute, Mister . . ."

"Agent Twiddy."

Jeff hitched his thumbs in the waistband of his jeans, chin tilted up. "Well, we sure as hell didn't have nothing to do with it, if that's the case. We never even got up that close to that crazy old woman."

Balls nodded like he understood perfectly and more or less agreed with the Cummins brothers. "Tell me," Balls said, "can you think of anyone maybe had reason to do this woman harm, maybe get in an argument with her, and hurt her real bad? Anyone dislike her that much?"

Jeff puffed out what sounded like a short chortle, but with no humor in it at all. "Well, I'll tell you, Agent Twiddy, I'd say a good half the folks what live all the way from Mann's Harbor to East Lake and down as far as Stumpy Point—half the folks—had no use at all for that crazy woman. I reckon a good half of 'em would like to see somebody get rid of her."

Robert laughed at his brother's words; then looked embarrassed as if he knew his laughing was not the thing to do. A sheepish expression came across his face and he cast his eyes to the ground.

None of this exchange seemed to register with Balls. The same bland expression—or lack of expression—remained on his countenance. "What I wonder is, one, when's the last time you saw her alive, and, two, whether you've seen anyone else come up here to be with her, see her."

Jeff took a breath. "I don't even know, exactly, when's the last time we seen her." He turned toward Robert. "You remember when we seen her last? I mean alive."

Robert shook his head. "Naw, I sure don't. Been three or four weeks or more I reckon."

Balls looked at first one, then the other. "What about visitors? You see folks come out here to see her?"

Jeff shook his head. "Not hardly any. Ever once in a while we seen that white van the women drive who brings her stuff. You know, food and clothes and stuff. Those do-gooder women."

Balls nodded.

Robert spoke up. "Not long ago, though, we did see that fancy Jeep or whatever it was come up the little road out there."

"Oh, that's right," Jeff said. "We was out hunting closer to the highway. We was a pretty fair piece away but we did see this Jeep or whatever come on to her road." He appeared to be trying to remember. "That was last week. Whether it went all the way down the road to her place, I don't know." He paused again for a moment. "But we're not as close to her place here as Wyatt. We live on the other side of him. So he'd be more'n likely to see somebody than us."

Balls remained quiet. Then he pressed both hands into the small of his back, stretching again. "Appreciate you two talking to me. Give your full names and phone numbers to Chief Deputy Wright there." He flexed his shoulders as if to loosen the muscles. "You boys can run along now. If we need to talk with you anymore, we know where to reach you."

Jeff Cummins eyed Balls. The look was not exactly unfriendly or aggressive. But it wasn't a look you'd give a friend you were getting ready to leave. Robert, though, grinned like he had enjoyed it all.

They turned to leave and Balls suddenly said, "Oh, just a minute. I know you boys do some fishing and construction work . . ."

"We're real good at framing," Robert said again.

"But what I'd like to know," Balls said, "if you do any farming?"

Jeff kept his eyes on Balls. "Whadda you mean?"

"You know, growing some things back there in the woods you shouldn't be growing."

Robert's eyes went wide and he looked at Jeff, at Balls, and back at Jeff.

Jeff was silent, staring, eyes boring into Balls.

Still sounding more or less friendly, Balls said, "Well, there was some young fellows came down from Virginia Beach the other night—couple of 'em still in jail—and they was headed your way. Had some drugs and stuff." He pursed his lips, ducked his head a bit, a sorrowful expression on his face. "Just don't want you boys to get into any trouble." He grinned really big at them. "Tell you what, I'll swing by your place in the next day or two. Make sure you're all right." The look now serious again, just like that. "You can run along now."

They hurried away. I thought they might run they moved so fast.

Odell came over to Balls.

Balls chuckled, shook his head. "In just a little while," he said, "I expect we're gonna see some smoke rising over those pine trees." Again the chuckle. "They're gonna be plowing under and burning stuff fast as they can."

"Growing?" Odell said.

"I'm sure of it," Balls said.

When the Cummins were out of sight, Deputy Duval came up to Odell and Balls. "I was looking around this morning earlier and just a little while ago, and that digging you said was up there in the clearing, that's not the only digging been going on around here. There are at least four other places I've seen where somebody dug quite a bit, and then mostly covered it up."

Odell appeared to ponder this. "Could be any number of reasons—from looking for fishing worms to burying garbage."

"Yep," Duval said, "I agree. But in looking around I went to that little lean-to at the back end of the trailer. She has a yard rake there with bent tines, a trowel or two and a plastic bucket, some other junky small tools." He cocked his head, looking first at Odell, then Balls, and back to Odell.

"But there's no shovel back there," he said. "No sign of one."

Chapter Twenty-Seven

I knew Balls was thinking the same thing I was—that a missing shovel was probably what was used to strike the Bear Woman in the back of the head. The edge of a shovel blade to the back of the head, swung by someone with plenty of strength, would be enough to kill a person.

Balls was silent.

Odell said, "Thanks, Duval. Glad you looked around. Good work."

Balls stood near the steps of the trailer. "You still got the key with you, Odell? Let's take a look around inside." Balls slipped on a pair of latex gloves. "You got an extra pair for him?" he said.

"Yep," Odell said, and fished in his side pocket and handed me a pair of the gloves. He donned a pair himself. He began to unlock the trailer. "Key for the car's hanging just inside the door, Duval. Saw it last time. See if you can start that car of hers."

"Okay," Duval said. He followed us to the entrance and when Odell stepped inside, he reached around and plucked the car keys and tossed them to Duval. Balls came in right behind Odell and I was next.

The first thing that hit me was the musty, closed up smell of the place. It wasn't a bad odor. Just sun baked and shut away. At the far end on the right a small bunk bed with quilts piled around. A sink with a few dishes in it was in the center of the trailer, a small two-burner propane stove next to the sink, a tiny refrigerator, the door open, and stocked with canned goods, obviously used more for storage than for keeping items cold. A bathroom was at the far left end of the trailer. Behind me, against the wall, were a table and chair. A space on the table was cleared enough for eating, but most of the table appeared to be used as a desk. Neatly stacked school-type notebooks and sheets of paper took up one end of the table. The stack of papers measured at least a foot or more in height. Several pencils and pens were upright in a mug beside the papers and notebooks. A dusty lamp sat on the other end of the table. Three other small lamps were placed around inside, one of them on the bookcase adjacent to the bed.

Balls went to the sink and tried the water. He turned the faucet and a spurt of water burped out. Balls looked around. He flipped a light switch and the overhead bulb glowed. "Water and electricity. All the comforts of home," he said. "Except no telephone and no TV."

"But there's a radio," I said. A tabletop radio was next to the bed. I turned the radio on briefly. It was set to FM 90.9, the classical music station. While Balls and Odell moved carefully around the trailer, I glanced at her books: A collection of Emily Dickinson's poems; Thoreau's *Walden*; Emerson essays; and several other books of poetry. The only novel was Sylvia Plath's *The Bell Jar*. I realized I was getting a different picture of the Bear Woman. She was becoming a real person to me, not just some vaguely deranged person who befriended bears and lived alone in the woods. Here was a woman who listened to classical music and read poetry and other books of substance. A woman who had left a marriage to choose this life for herself. But who knew what that marriage was like. Obviously it didn't suit her.

Balls and Odell were talking to each other but I wasn't paying attention to what they were saying. We heard the woman's car start, and Duval gently revved the engine a couple of times.

Odell stood near the open door. "Okay, Duval," he called. "Cut it off."

With his eyes, Balls made one more sweep around the interior. "I'll get the lab boys to go over the inside here and see if she had any visitors. Kind a doubt it. But we'll check."

He came over to the table and lifted a few of the papers in the stack. Most appeared to be musings or notes, written out in longhand with a pen, but a few were in pencil.

I stood beside him. "You want me to take that stack of papers and notebooks home and look at them, go through them, see if there's anything of interest?"

Balls frowned at me, thinking. He slanted his head to one side and appeared ready to say something, which I figured would be a negative.

But Odell spoke up. "Could be a big help. Bring Weav on as a consultant or something."

"I guess that's an option." Balls said. "Okay, hotshot, you can take this with you, go through it, but you damn well better not let anything happen to it." He gave his shoulders a shrug. "Don't let that bird of yours crap on any of the pages."

"I'll bring it back in perfect condition and order," I said. Lifting the stack, I carried it cradled in my arm out to the cruiser, opened the back door and snugged the stack against the seat where I could hold it when we drove back.

Balls and Odell stepped out of the trailer and Odell locked the door behind them. Both of them peeled off their gloves and stuck them in their pockets. I looked at my hands. Peeled my gloves off and did the same.

Duval spoke to Odell. "The battery's a little weak. But her car started up okay."

"We heard it."

"Little more'n a quarter a tank of gas in it." Duval handed Odell the car keys. "I locked it up."

I approached Balls. "Surprised we haven't had any reporters out here yet."

"We will have soon enough," Balls said. "The sheriff's got to announce this as a homicide at some point real soon, if he hasn't already." He stared at the ground, chewing his lower lip. "We still don't know whether there're any relatives, and it doesn't appear there are. There's just that ex-husband." He puffed out a breath of air. More to Odell than to me, he said, "I guess I'd better inform the ex before the press does. We owe him that much, I suppose."

"Meanwhile," Odell said, "what would you like me to do?"

"We've got to talk to those three some more—Wilkinson and the Cummins brothers. And see if they don't know of some other neighbors this woman may have pissed off."

"I'll run you—and Weav—back to Manteo and then I'll come back here and hunt up those three again. They're not far away. And get some more names."

Balls sighed. "I expect there's gonna be a whole lot of folks around here we'll wanna talk to."

Odell studied Balls' face. "What's your gut feeling about this . . . this case?"

"For the moment, and that's just for right now, I'd say she finally riled one of these good ol' boys—not necessarily any of the three we've talked to—enough that he'd had as much as he could take . . . and he whacked her a good one."

Odell nodded. "That would seem the most likely scenario."

We started walking toward the cruiser. Balls stopped and turned to Odell. "But I learned a long time ago that the 'most likely scenario' ain't necessarily the right one."

Chapter Twenty-Eight

As we prepared to get in the cruiser, Balls stopped with the passenger door open. "Hey, Odell," he called, "just look a there." He pointed to the west.

Just beyond the pine trees a thin wisp of smoke arose, dispersing in the light wind.

Odell grinned. "Right on, Agent Twiddy. Right on."

We drove back to Manteo and Odell dropped Balls and me off at the courthouse. He'd pulled to a stop right beside Balls' car. "I'll head right on back," Odell said, "and I'll touch base with you tonight."

Balls nodded, and he and I got in his Thunderbird. It was awkward for me as I cradled the stack of papers and notebooks. I had to be careful with them as I squirmed to fasten my seat belt. Balls glanced at me as he buckled his seatbelt. "Sorry you don't have time to go in and see your sweetie, but you may be going to see her tomorrow just to check on that property the woman lived on. Her ex says it's hers. I wanta make sure. See what the Register of Deeds' records say."

"Will do," I said.

Balls checked the stack of papers in my lap. "You got a lot of reading to go through there, cowboy."

"Be interesting, I think. Who knows, may shed some light that will help us."

He headed to the highway and out of town. "What's this 'us' business? I may be letting you hang around as my Lucky Charm, but just remember there ain't no 'us' in this investigation."

I smiled and nodded. "Yes sir, Agent Twiddy."

He gave his head a shake. "For the life of me, I can't see what a pretty gal like that Elly Pedersen sees in a beat up old newspaper guy like you."

"I'm not that beat up."

"Got wrinkles on your face. Getting a few gray hairs on the sides. How much older are you than her, anyway?"

"Only a few years."

"Yeah. How many's a few?" He turned left at the stoplight and headed at a shade over fifty-five to the Washington Baum Bridge over Roanoke Sound.

I was quiet and looked out at the sound. There was hardly any wind and the water was smooth, flat. Unusually smooth. The mood of the water varied every time I crossed one of the bridges. The water was governed by the wind, sun, and time of day. I always wished I could name the colors of the water. To me, today it was sort of a blue-gray except for different channels or bands of water that reflected a washed out purple from the sky. Then I answered Balls. "Eight years. Almost nine."

"She's a mere child. Don't you feel guilty?"

I chuckled. "Not in the least," I said and added after a beat or two: "She's not a child exactly, Balls. She's got a little boy five years old. And she was married for a couple of years before her husband died."

"Pushing thirty then," Balls said. "Makes you pushing forty."

I chuckled again. "And how old are you, Balls?"

"None of your damn business."

"But everybody else's age is your business."

"I'm an investigator." He grinned. He loved it.

When we came to the end of the bridge and entered

Nags Head, he slowed to a shade over fifty. We continued up the Bypass to Kill Devil Hills, and he made a left at Third Street. His cell phone chirped and he pulled to the side of the road, stopped and fished the cell out of his belt. "Yeah?" He listened and then said, "Ten o'clock. Okay, will be there. Thanks." He signed off and puffed out a breath of air.

I looked at him inquisitively.

"The sheriff's holding a press conference tomorrow morning at ten at the courthouse. I've been wondering when the press was going to zero in on this."

"He'll announce that it is a homicide?" I asked.

"He's going to have to," Balls said. He checked the rear-view mirror and then eased the car forward. "Your friend Linda Shackleford from *The Coastland Times* is the one that requested a press conference."

Balls drove slowly down to Bay Drive and turned toward Devon Sasser's house. He pulled into the driveway just as Devon was reaching in the back of his boxy, dark-colored Nissan SUV. Apparently he had arrived shortly before we came up. He was dressed in what we would describe at the Outer Banks as casual business attire—creased slacks, a collared, long-sleeve subdued sport shirt. He retrieved a sample business case and set it on the ground as he turned toward us, an inquisitive frown that he directed at us. He canted that little round head of his toward us as we got out of the car. His glasses caught a shaft of light. I thought again how his long and lanky, somewhat muscular body, didn't seem to belong to that small, round face and head.

Balls managed to get out of the car before I did because I had to be careful with the stack of papers, placing them on the seat I was vacating.

Devon took several steps toward us. "Yeah?" he said, a certain wariness in his voice as if he were afraid we brought more bad news. Then he managed to give something of a practiced smile, but it didn't last. "More news?" he said. "I didn't really expect to see you . . ." His voice trailed off.

Balls extended his hand and they shook briefly. "I'm afraid I do have some news, Mr. Sasser, and I wanted to give you the information before you read it in the paper or heard it over TV."

Devon remained motionless, his long arms hanging by his side. It was not a relaxed stance, though. There was a coiled tension about the way he stood.

Balls kept his eyes on Devon as he spoke. "The medical examiner has determined that your ex-wife was not killed by the bears but that she was killed by a human being."

"What? Whatta you mean, killed by a human being?"

"Yes," Balls said rather formally, "we're now investigating her death as a homicide."

"You mean she was murdered?"

"Her death was obviously a homicide. 'Murder' is a legal term. Right now we classify it as a homicide. Nothing more."

Devon cast his eyes on the ground. Then he looked back up at Balls. "How was she . . . how killed? Was she shot?"

"No, the medical examiner says she was hit with something. Not shot." Before Devon could say anything else, and he appeared ready to speak, Balls said, "The reason I wanted to inform you of this is because tomorrow morning Sheriff Albright is having a press conference at which he will tell reporters that the death of Estelle Byerly Sasser, known as the 'Bear Woman' is being investigated as a homicide. And as I said, I didn't want you to learn about this from news accounts. I figured you—as her ex-husband—should know this in advance." Then he added more quietly, "And we haven't been able to find any other people—relatives—connected to her."

Devon flexed his fingers, then clinched them loosely again into fists. "Some of those guys what live near her. She was always pissing them off. Screaming at them if they got near her damn bears. They've got to be the ones what done her in." He lifted his chin and nodded vigorously. "I always figured those guys would get enough of her."

Balls listened to him, all the while studying his face. "We're investigating all possibilities."

Devon acknowledged Balls' words. "That press conference. When is it?"

"Ten o'clock tomorrow morning at the courthouse in Manteo."

Devon seemed to weigh the information. Then he said, "I was going back to Rocky Mount tomorrow to follow up on a call, but I want to hear what the sheriff has to say." He looked at Balls. "You don't have to be a reporter to go to the press conference, do you?"

"I'm sure there'd be no problem with you attending," Balls said. "As I said, I wanted to let you know before you heard it on the news."

"Appreciate it." He gave quick bob of his head. The long scratch along his face had healed nicely but it was going to leave a faint scar for a few weeks at any rate.

As Balls and I got into his car to leave, I looked back at Devon's house. It was neat and looked orderly and well kept. The door to the garage, with its utility room, was open and I could see how neatly stowed everything was in there.

Balls didn't have anything to say as he drove slowly out of the neighborhood and headed toward my house. He was obviously doing serious thinking. In fact, he was so deep in thought he almost missed my cul-de-sac.

"You turn here, Balls."

"Yeah. Sure." He pulled close to the carport and sat there a moment. Not really looking at me, he said, "What'd you think of Devon's reaction to the news?"

I had thought about it. "He was quick to figure it was one of her neighbors, the guys she antagonizes."

"Yeah," he said, "that's what most people will assume." He drummed the fingers on one hand on the steering wheel. "That's the obvious."

I knew exactly what was going through his mind.

I glanced over at Balls' profile. "So what's the 'not so obvious'?"

He shook his head and sighed. "I don't know yet." He puffed out a breath of air. "I gotta go."

"You staying here tonight?"

"Yeah, damn it. Like to get home, but doesn't make any sense. Not with the press conference in the morning, and I'm going to go back out there probably before dark, see what Odell may have come up with. Obvious or not, I know I'm going to be having some real serious talks with that Wilkinson neighbor and the Cummins boys. Probably some others."

"Sorry you won't see Lorraine tonight."

"Yeah, me too." He flipped a palm toward the stack of papers in my lap. "Maybe you'll run across something in there that's useful." As an afterthought, he reached over and opened the glove compartment, took out a pair of latex gloves. "Wear these when you go through those papers. Just in case."

I nodded. "I want to go through it as much as I can this afternoon and tonight. I'd like to get through most of it before the press conference tomorrow." I opened the passenger door. "I'll see you at the courthouse in the morning."

"No visiting with your sweetie tonight . . . either," he said.

"I'll call her." Then I said, more to myself, "And also call my editor. She'll be excited . . . now that it's a homicide."

"Keep a lid on it," he said.

"I will. Just want to give my editor a heads up." I got out of the car, cradling the stack of papers in both arms and used a bump from my hip to close the door.

He backed the Thunderbird out of the driveway and swung around in the circular cul-de-sac, ready to head back out to the Bypass and beyond. He had a frown on his face, thinking hard, and I knew trying to come up with something that was on the other side of the obvious.

Chapter Twenty-Nine

When I got inside my house the first thing I did, after care-fully depositing the stack of the Bear Woman's papers on my desk, was to quickly check on Janey, and go to the phone to call Rose, my editor in New York.

Rose answered with a cough and her heavy Brooklyn accent.

"I've got the makings for another good story for you, Rose," I said.

"Yeah, Weaver, you got more mayhem down there in Magnoliaville?"

I told her about the Bear Woman and her death.

Rose listened with very few comments. I could tell that from time to time she took a drag on one of her constant cig-arettes.

When I'd finished, she said, "Jesus. Any suspects? Ar-rests?"

"No, not yet, but I wanted to give you a heads up on it."

"I tell you, Weaver, you just keep on finding bodies down there and before long you're going to have half the population done away with." She gave out one of her cackles infused with coughs. "This is why you're one of my favorite writers."

"I thought I was *the* favorite writer, period." We went through this routine almost every time we talked.

"Well you are, honey-bunch . . . Isn't that what they say in the South?"

"I'm not honey-bunch. I'm sweetie-pie."

She cackled again. "I can't keep all these terms straight." Then more seriously, "Keep me posted on the Bear Woman. That has the makings of a hell of a story. Double-length magazine piece if not another book."

When we signed off, I called Elly to bring her up-to-date and tell her that, while we had planned to be together tonight, I needed to bury myself in the Bear Woman's papers. Toward the end of my rather detailed report, I told her about our visit to Devon Sasser to inform him that his ex-wife's death was being investigated as a homicide.

She said, "I knew his name but I'd never met him or seen him to my knowledge—until Friday or the day before. Can't remember exactly."

That got my attention real quick.

"You saw Devon Sasser? At the Register of Deeds?"

"I just saw him and heard his name. Janet helped him with the records. He was looking up the property that Estelle Byerly Sasser has . . . or had, I guess, since she died—or was killed."

"What did he want to know?"

"I only heard part of the conversation, but he wanted to check how the deed was registered. Before their divorce it was apparently in both of their names. After the divorce—and that was twenty or more years ago—it was just in her name." She paused a moment. "I assume he wanted to know whether the land—thirty-four acres—would come back to him since she didn't have any next of kin."

"He asked Janet this?"

"Yes, but she told him that was a legal question and she couldn't be of any help on that. She could just show him the records."

We talked a bit longer and then she said, "Well, I guess I'd better let you get to the reading of those papers."

"Yes, it's quite a stack. Not sure I'll get all the way through tonight."

"Don't forget to eat," she said.

I smiled. I couldn't let her go without saying, "I love you, Elly."

"I love you too."

I sat there a moment longer, then cast my eyes toward that pile of papers on my desk. Giving out an audible sigh, I eased myself out of the chair and went to the desk to begin plowing through those papers.

I'll admit that I sat there for several minutes simply staring dumbly at the stack of papers—and probably sighing mightily. A daunting task, I felt, not so much by the sheer volume of scribbled material but the fact that I wanted to do it justice. This was a woman's life, all that was left of it. Of course, there was the off chance the words might shed some light on the overall investigation, but that was really a long shot. A very long shot. Except for the small collection of books in her trailer, the worn down trailer itself, and the equally worn down automobile, these papers, as far as we knew, were the sum total of her twenty-some years in the relative wilderness.

So, slipping on the latex gloves, I took another deep breath and started.

Chapter Thirty

Pulling out the notebooks from the bottom of the stack, I figured I would start with those. They were like college notebooks, bound, with semi-hard covers that were mottled in black and white like slabs of marble. A quick glance through the notebooks told me that they were in chronological order, with the one on the very bottom the first one she had written in. And her cursive handwriting was neat and easy to read. Most of the notations were done with a pen, probably a ballpoint. Only a few parts were in pencil, which had faded slightly.

Obviously these were journals of her contact with the bears. The earliest ones had dates when she had sighted the bears. Admittedly, I skimmed through some of the notations in order to get a sense of the flow and the progress she had made in befriending the bears.

At one point, well into the second year, she acknowledged she had fed the bears and in the same note she added that she knew full well that feeding the bears was frowned on; in fact, it was prohibited. But she wrote that she knew of no other way to get the bears to recognize her as a friend.

It was September of her third year living there in the woods that she wrote:

Today one of the bears came within seven or

eight yards of me. I was thrilled. I stood perfectly
still. He sniffed the air. I held out my hand with
food. The food was a glob of peanut butter and
honey. Very slowly I bent over and placed the food
on the ground. The bear stared at me. I couldn't tell
whether he might charge. I slowly stood up straight,
spoke softly and then took measured steps back-
ward. Finally, I turned around and retreated to the
far side of the pasture. The bear had not moved.
Then he came forward to the food, and I left him
there so he could eat without my presence.

According to her journals, after that first encounter with
the bear, the sightings and approach of the bears became
more frequent. One bear in particular approached her more
than the others.

The first three notebooks were filled with reports about
the bears and how they became more used to her. The last
entry in the third notebook was made less than a year ago.
Using exclamation points quite liberally, she wrote that one
of the older male bears—she had named him Cyrano because
he had an unusually long snout—came so close to her that
she could smell him, and actually was close enough to reach
out and touch him. She didn't write whether she touched
him.

Apparently, she had run out of notebooks because her
notations about the bears from that point on were made on
loose sheets of lined paper.

I did take special interest in several notations over the
years when she had written that she had to yell at "intruders"—apparently neighbors or hunters—who came too close
to "my bears." However, she never gave names of these
intruders; whether she even knew their names, I had no idea.

A fourth notebook was somewhat buried near the top of
the loose sheets of paper. It was not about the bears at all.
With a heavy magic marker, she had hand printed in big

block letters on the outside of the notebook "Poetry."

I decided that would be the next notebook I would go through. But I realized, too, that my shoulders felt stiff and my back ached a bit. Checking the time, I saw that it was a couple of minutes before nine o'clock. Had no idea the time had gone so fast. And I hadn't eaten. I stood up and stretched. When I did, I could certainly tell that I had sat there at my desk for quite a while. I peeled off the gloves and laid them on the stack of papers. Even Janey had been silent and probably wondered why I hadn't covered her cage. She chirped once, rather disheartedly.

"Okay," I said. "I know, you wonder why it is so quiet. Time for you to get covered up and go to sleep properly."

Also, I realized it was time for me to eat something. Past time, really. I decided to cover Janey's cage after I had fixed a little dinner for myself. She enjoyed the activity of my moving around in the kitchen and any sort of noise I might make with pots and pans.

No pots and pans tonight, however. I decided on almost the same supper as I had had—when?—last night. I split three saved biscuits, put American cheese on them, popped them in the toaster oven, while I fixed a bowl of Cascadian Farm Organic cereal, the French vanilla and almond flavored I had left. Added a bit of sugar and whole milk. No watered down milk for me; I didn't drink that much milk, and when I did, I wanted the real thing.

The hot toasted cheese biscuits and cereal hit the spot. Good supper for me, and I went back to the Bear Woman's papers.

I was pretty well satisfied with the account of contact with the bears. Sure, there were details I could read more thoroughly but I was convinced I had the overall picture firmly fixed. I put the gloves on, ready to begin the task again.

So I picked up the poetry notebook I had put down before eating. In it, the woman had obviously copied some of her favorite poems. Toward the back of the notebook there were poems she had written and dated. Inserted at the back, too, were drafts of poems she was writing but were apparently not in a final form she liked. I planned to go through her originals and the drafts later. First I was curious to see what poems she had copied in the front of the book.

Quite appropriately I thought, the first poem in the book, copied in her neat hand, was Robert Frost's "The Road Not Taken." Well, Estelle Byerly had certainly taken "the road less traveled."

Following Frost's poem there were several she had copied by Emily Dickinson, which she obviously loved. (But not one of my personal favorite poets.) These were followed by several poets I wasn't familiar with. Then a few pages later she had copied the final verse or stanza of William Cullen Bryant's "Thanatopsis," the one many high school students were required to memorize:

So live, that when thy summons comes to join
The innumerable caravan, which moves
To that mysterious realm, where each shall take
His chamber in the silent halls of death,
Thou go not, like the quarry-slave at night,
Scourged to his dungeon, but, sustained and soothed
By an unfaltering trust, approach thy grave,
Like one who wraps the drapery of his couch
About him, and lies down to pleasant dreams.

I had to smile to myself with the irony by what she had written next. Adjacent to this segment of "Thanatopsis" were the lines of a poem Dylan Thomas had penned to his dying father:

And now, my father, there on the sad height,
Curse, bless me now with your fierce tears, I pray.
Do not go gentle into that good night.

Rage, rage against the dying of the light.

Next to "Thanatopsis," the Bear Woman had written "No!" and beside the Dylan Thomas lines she had "Yes!" Well, the Bear Woman had certainly not gone "gentle into that good night."

I felt even more like she was becoming a real person to me.

I decided to come back to the poetry notebook after I'd gone through the loose papers on top.

The first thing I noticed about the loose papers was the handwriting. It had become less neat. Some of the words were actually difficult to make out. The lines of cursive writing slanted down to the right. It did not seem like her handwriting that I had seen in the earlier notebooks. She made it easy because virtually every paper was dated. Some with just the year, but most had at least month and year. Those on top were obviously the most recent musings and observations. In some she described the weather, if it was unusual, and she also waxed a bit eloquent, and even poetic, about sunrises and sunsets.

There were several notations regarding when the Good Samaritan women had brought her supplies. Then she had scribbled tirades against the "men nearby" who threatened her and her bears. "They call me a crazy bitch" she wrote, and added in big bold writing "I think they are planning against me."

While I had come to feel like I knew her better as I read through the material—and she was no longer the "Bear Woman," but Estelle in my mind—I couldn't help but sense a degree of sadness as I realized she was deteriorating. Not just her handwriting, but in the way her mind was functioning. As Shakespeare wrote in one of his plays and had used as a recurring theme on more than one occasion: "Oh, what a falling off was there." And this was obvious the closer I came to present day.

Near the top of the stack I discovered a business envelope, not sealed, and on the outside of the envelope she had printed in wobbly block letters: "Upon my death."

I stared at the envelope for several moments, holding it in my hands. I wasn't sure I wanted to read the contents, but knew I had to and most certainly would. Carefully I opened the envelope and took out the tri-folded single sheet of paper. At the top of the page she had written "Last Will and Testament." A simple one sentence followed: "I leave my land, all thirty-four acres, along with any possessions of mine, to the local Nature Conservancy." She had dated the page a year ago and signed her name, "Estelle Byerly." She had left off the "Sasser." I refolded the sheet of paper and inserted it in the envelope. I put the envelope to one side. As I did so, a small wry smile crept across my face. Well, Devon, I'm no lawyer but it looks like to me there goes any chance you might have at getting possession of this land.

Then I stood, stretched and walked about the living room, flexing my shoulders and my arms. Sat back down and took the last inch or so of loose papers. Some had only a few lines scribbled on them; others were filled front and part of the back. It saddened me to look at these because they reflected a changed Estelle Byerly. It was clear that she was becoming more paranoid about the neighbors and life in general.

Near the top of the stack she had copied part of a poem by Thomas Bailey Aldrich called "Memory." She had written:

My mind lets go a thousand things
Like dates of wars and deaths of kings,
And yet recalls the very hour—
'Twas noon by yonder village tower
And on the last blue noon in May—

Then following the poem she had added verses of her

own. In a scrawling hand she wrote:

> *But my mind won't let go of a deed so horrid*
> *It drives sharp nails into my forehead.*
> *The memory is there, not buried so deep*
> *As the one who 'neath the soil does sleep.*
> *Decades so long she does sleep, sleep, sleep*
> *I can no longer let her lie so deep . . .*

There were more words that were so sloppily written I couldn't make them out.

In one of my own notebooks, I carefully copied this page of hers—the fragment of Thomas Bailey Aldrich's poem and the verses she had added, and added in her tortured handwriting. I didn't try to copy the other words she had scrawled there since I couldn't make them out anyway. Why had I done it? It was difficult to explain to myself, so I thought about it, and soon realized that the other comments she had written were simply single words, like good, bad, yes, and no. And then the verses she had penned were the usual topics—beautiful sunsets, full moons, the majesty of bears. That sort of thing. This was the only verse she had written with a strong, seething passion, or torment. I felt it was worth keeping and pondering over.

In a sense, I knew that these lines were truly her "last will and testament."

I felt they held a secret. A deep, dark secret.

But what?

Chapter Thirty-One

It was shortly after midnight when I went to bed. Sleep didn't come right away. In fact, sleep didn't come for quite a while. I lay there and thought about Estelle Byerly, the Bear Woman. But I no longer thought of her as just the Bear Woman. I felt as though I had traveled with her from those first years when she chose the wilderness and the bears, and did so with an obvious degree of contentment, until these later years when she became more and more tortured over something, and her mind began to take on dimensions that were not there in the earlier years.

One of the last pages of hers I had read bore the sentence that haunted me: "I have no friends in this world except the bears. No one but the bears."

Too, there was some secret, I sensed, that she couldn't let go of.

Finally sleep came and I dreamed of woods and damp ground and at one point in the dream I glimpsed a bear with a long snout peering at me from the brush.

I awakened just before seven. My first thought, before I had even gotten out of bed, was of Estelle Byerly's final moments and her friendship with the bears. Knowing full well it was bizarre, I still had to wonder if perhaps her favorite bear, Cyrano, had dragged her lifeless body back to her home, the falling-down green trailer, and that the damage to her left shoulder was caused by the bear dragging her—not in ferocious anger, but in friendship. Taking her home.

I shook my head and got up. After a shower and getting dressed, I retrieved a cardboard box from the utility room off the carport that was a perfect size to use for transporting the woman's papers. I put the envelope with her handwritten will on the top of the stack in the box.

I arrived at the courthouse before nine, and carried the box with the papers upstairs. Balls and Odell sat talking quietly in the interrogation room. Balls looked up at me and nodded me in. I set the box on the table before them and took the third chair.

Balls canted his head at the box. "Anything interesting?"

"Yes," I said. "Somewhat." Waiting a beat or two, I added, "That's her handwritten will in the envelope on top."

Balls picked up the envelope carefully by the edges. "You use gloves when you went through this stuff?" I nodded. He wasn't wearing gloves. "Well my prints are on file in case there's any question." He opened the envelope and read the brief sentence. That half-smile of his appeared. He held the letter by its edges so Odell could read it. "Looks like good old ex-husband Devon Sasser is left out in the cold."

Odell leaned forward so he could see the top papers in the box. I turned the box toward them so they wouldn't have to read upside down. After the envelope, the next sheet of paper was the one on which she had written about having no friends but the bears. I started to say something about how—just perhaps—one of the bears had dragged her back to the trailer after she was dead, but I decided not to. I did, however, comment about how I was convinced that her mind had begun to go toward the end. I said I could tell it in her handwriting and by what she wrote.

Balls made that dismissive pursing of his lips. "Living out there in the woods for twenty years with nothing but a bunch of damn black bears would do it."

Odell lifted that sheet of paper by its edges and then

looked carefully at the next one. It was the partial Aldrich poem with the opening line, "My mind lets go a thousand things . . ." He stared at the page for quite a while. I looked at the expression on his face as he read her scribbled verses following the poem. He suddenly looked deflated like the air had gone out of his body.

"What is it?" I asked softly.

"Oh, nothing, I don't guess . . ."

I leaned toward him, my arms resting on the table. "Really?"

Odell shrugged. "I guess it's the business about 'the last blue noon in May' and then all that stuff she'd written about a 'deed most horrid.' That got to me a little."

I looked at him quizzically. "Yes?"

Balls was quiet. He watched Odell, then me.

Odell stared at me a moment before he spoke. "It just sort of reminded me, you know. It was a pretty day in May— you could say the 'last blue noon in May' because the weather really got nasty the next day—when Luanne disappeared." He shook his head as if to rid it of images, and attempted something of a smile. "And that was certainly a 'deed most horrid.'"

Balls cleared his throat. "We might as well go downstairs. The sheriff wants us there. Press conference'll be starting before too long. And we need to brief the sheriff . . . with what damn little we know."

"These papers?" I said.

Odell said, "I'll lock 'em up. Secure them."

The three of us met with Sheriff Eugene Albright downstairs. He was overseeing setting up for the press conference. Deputy Dorsey was moving chairs around, lining up six of them in the front near the podium. Mabel stood to one side, giving instructions, I was sure.

Sheriff Albright is a big man, a full face and sandy-gray thinning hair, his frame tending toward a comfortable portliness. I've always felt he would rather counsel a young man rather than lock him up. Basically a gentle soul.

The sheriff greeted me with a smile and a handshake, and then addressed Balls and Odell. "I'll give a brief opening statement, telling the reporters that it is a homicide and that it is being investigated as such. Then I'm going to turn it over to you two."

"Yes, sir," Odell said.

"That's fine," Balls said. "Of course, we ain't gonna be able to tell them much." He looked at the chairs in front. There was space in the back for non-media people to stand or sit. "How many reporters are you expecting?"

"Linda Shackleford for certain. And Neel Keller of *The Outer Banks Sentinel*. Then someone covering for *The Virginian-Pilot*. A radio reporter, and even a two-person crew from one of the Norfolk TV stations." He hunched his hefty shoulders in a sort of shrug. "Maybe others, but I think that'll be about it."

I checked the time. It was twenty minutes to ten. I stepped away to speak to Mabel. She's always got a kindly smile. She spoke to me, then turned toward Albright. "Sheriff, I'll be in the back if you need me."

"Thank you, Mabel."

I had time to slip by Elly's office and at least say hello.

I took the stairs hurriedly and went into Elly's office. She looked lovely and fresh as always. She has a way of training her hazel eyes on me that make me feel like she's sending me a secret message. "If we're not busy, I'm going to try to slip into the press conference once it gets started, there in the back."

I touched her hand, smiled, and tried to send her a secret message with my eyes. Maybe I did because she smiled in return and gave something of a tiny mischievous wink.

Back upstairs, I took a seat near the front but behind the row of chairs for the working media. Linda Shackleford came in first. I stood and shook hands with her. She's got a solid grip. "You're not sitting up here?" she said, indicating the row of seats up front.

"No, that's for you legitimate folks."

She grinned, displaying her big, strong white teeth.

The other reporters came in. The radio newsman put a small recorder on the podium before taking a seat. He held another recorder in his hand. A TV reporter I'd seen on one of the Norfolk news shows came in, sat, and looked back at his cameraman, who supported a video camera on his right shoulder. A padded microphone, attached to the top of the camera, aimed toward the podium. The cameraman was positioned so he could aim at the podium and frame his colleague in the picture as well.

At two minutes past ten, Sheriff Albright stepped up to the podium. Balls and Odell stood tall and straight just a pace or two from his right and slightly behind. Albright was in a freshly pressed and starched uniform, minus only a tie. He glanced down at notes lying on the podium. He cleared his throat and looked up at the reporters. "Thank you for coming today. I'll have a brief statement and then turn the questions over to SBI Agent Ballsford Twiddy and to Dare County Sheriff's Department Chief Deputy Odell Wright. They are the lead investigators on this . . ." He started to say "investigation" but changed it to ". . . on this case." He cleared his throat again. "As you have heard, I know, we are investigating the death of Estelle Byerly Sasser, known to many people only as the 'Bear Woman.' No disrespect intended. Contrary to what was believed initially, Mrs. Sasser was not killed by one or more of the bears she befriended. She was killed by a blow to the head." He paused.

The reporter from *The Virginian-Pilot* raised her hand but spoke out immediately. "How do you know it was *not* a bear?"

Sheriff Albright frowned, then managed a more pleasant expression. "As I said, she was killed with a blow to the head." He actually smiled as he said, "No bear is going to wield an object that inflicts a blow to the head."

The TV reporter said, "What about suspects, Sheriff? Have you made any arrests?"

Albright said, "We've just started the investigation. No arrests at this time."

"But what about suspects?" the TV reporter said.

Sheriff Albright hesitated a moment, glanced to his right at Balls, and said, "That concludes my statement. I'm going to ask SBI Agent Twiddy to take over. He's the lead investigator on this." He started to step away from the podium, and then added, ". . . assisted by Chief Deputy Wright." He moved to his left and Balls took a step to the podium.

I took a moment to glance quickly around the room. Elly stood at the back close to the door. She gave a faint smile when she saw me looking at her. Two other workers from the courthouse stood to her left, and then there was Devon Sasser, still and erect, his little round face and head perched atop that lanky, muscular frame of a body. Sitting up close, just a little distance from the reporters, was District Attorney Rick Schweikert, his close-cropped blondish hair brushed immaculately. As usual, he glared at me. No love lost.

Balls started to speak and my attention was back to the podium. "As the sheriff said, the investigation is just underway. We will be talking with a number of different people."

The TV reporter again: "In other words, you don't have any suspects. Any persons of interest?"

I could tell Balls struggled to keep his voice level, not let irritation show. "We will be talking with a number of people," he repeated.

Then Balls pointed to Linda Shackleford, who had her hand up. She said, "Can you tell us what she was hit in the head with?"

"Not at this time, other than she was killed with a blow to the head."

Another reporter, a young man from the Elizabeth City *Daily Advance,* who arrived just before the conference started, fired a question: "I've heard that she had been dead for several days before she was found. Is this correct, and if so, how could you tell she wasn't killed by the bears? I mean the condition of the body and everything."

Balls said, "The medical examiner in Greenville made the determination." He rubbed a palm across his chin, thinking. "I can tell you that there was some damage to her body —perhaps by animals—but these were inflicted postmortem according to the medical examiner."

Another question from *The Virginian Pilot* reporter: "How long had she lived in the woods near East Lake befriending those bears?"

Odell Wright moved a bit closer to Balls and the podium. Odell said, "She had lived there for more than twenty years, and had become quite friendly with the bears over the years."

Not to be outdone as a questioner, the TV reporter spoke out in his distinct on-camera voice, "You have no arrests and no suspects. How many other unsolved cases do you have in the county?"

Sheriff Albright stiffened visibly. He wasn't going to let this question slide. "This is *not* an unsolved case. We've just started the investigation. And as for our record of solving cases, we have a very good record . . ."

Schweikert couldn't stay quiet any longer—or still; he squirmed like ants were after him. "Sheriff, if I may, please, let me respond to that."

"By all means. Mr. Schweikert, our district attorney."

Schweikert stood tall, dressed to the nines in his stiffly starched white dress shirt and tie, the only one in the room with a tie. He stepped around front so he was facing the TV reporter—with the camera aimed at him over the reporter's shoulder. As he spoke, his voice was every bit as much "on-camera" as that of the TV reporter: "We have an outstanding record of arrests and convictions of those who commit crimes within this county. In fact, our success rate on solving—and prosecuting successfully—felonies is about the best in the state. The number of so-called 'unsolved' crimes over the past two decades can be counted as fewer than the fingers on one hand . . ."

I stole a look at Odell's face; I wanted to see his reaction when the subject was unsolved cases. Odell's face remained impassive, unreadable, but I knew he had to be thinking about his little sister.

Schweikert continued: "As the good sheriff said, this current case is most certainly not unsolved. It's just getting under investigation. I have all the confidence in the world that our investigators—the best around—will solve this heinous crime, the brutal slaying of a gentle soul known as the Bear Woman."

I knew he had to work the word "heinous" in somewhere. He's never talked about a crime here in the county that wasn't a "heinous crime."

The TV reporter seemed somewhat mollified. "Thank you," he said softly, not using his on-camera voice.

There were a number of other questions from the reporters, many of them repeats in various forms of what had already been asked.

As a windup question, Linda Shackleford asked, "Agent Twiddy or Chief Deputy Wright, can you tell us what is your next step?"

Balls nodded to Odell, and Odell stepped slightly forward. "Yes, Linda, we will be talking with some of the victim's neighbors. Determine whether they have noticed any unusual activity in the vicinity of the victim's trailer."

The reporter for the Elizabeth City *Daily Advance* shot his hand up almost before Odell got through speaking. "I understand that she was not popular at all with her neighbors. That she was very vocal in keeping them away from what she considered *her* bears."

Odell glanced at Balls who gave an almost imperceptible go-ahead look. Odell said, "That's true. There have been rumors of some animosity among the neighbors."

Balls didn't keep quiet. "But being unpopular doesn't by any means necessarily equate with killing." He softened his response with a chuckle. "If it did, if all of us were done in because we were unpopular or had offended someone at some time, I'm afraid most of us in this room would be running the risk of a similar fate."

There was a smattering of subdued laughter among the reporters and the audience.

Sheriff Albright stepped forward. "Ladies and gentlemen, I think that wraps up anything we are able to say at this juncture. We will keep you informed as we proceed."

The reporters shuffled their notebooks together and prepared to leave. The radio newsman retrieved his microphone from the podium. I glanced at the back of the room just as Elly had her hand on the door. A faint smile toward me and she exited.

Devon Sasser was already gone.

Chapter Thirty-Two

Very little happened on the investigation into Estelle Byerly's homicide the next several days—at least that I was privileged to. I'm sure Balls and Odell were working it, but I stayed out of their way for a change.

I had made three more calls to volunteers in the search for Luanne Wright twenty-two years ago that were totally fruitless. I still had not talked to Devon Sasser about his role in the search, but this was not the time for that. So, in effect, I'd sadly reached a sort of dead-end on Luanne's case—as if it hadn't been a dead-end when I started.

At a little past nine Saturday morning I stepped out on my deck, breathing in the fresh air and the tinge of salt coming in off the ocean, and called Elly. "Another lovely spring morning in paradise. Maybe you and Martin would like to take a little ride with me across the bridge . . . over toward East Lake."

There was a hint of teasing in her voice: "You can't let it go, can you?"

"I don't know what you mean?" Just as much of a tease in my voice.

"You know exactly what I mean." Then, "You're not planning to drive out to the woman's place, are you?"

"Oh, no. I expect Balls and Odell are out there now. Besides, it's cordoned off pretty well." I shifted the phone in my hand and watched a blue jay ignoring me to eat some of the seeds on the railing at the far end of the deck. "But I thought you might like to see where the little road is that leads to her place. Maybe stop at Stan's Market and get a snack."

She chuckled. "Sure, Mr. Crime Writer. I'll be sort of your sidekick and go with you. Besides, Martin always likes an adventure . . . and maybe some ice cream."

I drove to Manteo shortly after ten and continued through town toward the airport, turned left off the highway and then left again and pulled up to Elly's house. The sun sparkled. Trees had leafed out fully. Two little toy trucks were in the smoothed dirt under the spreading live oak tree where Martin and Lauren from next door played.

As I got out of my Outback, Elly stepped on to the porch near the steps. She smiled brightly and raised one hand, wiggling her fingers at me. She looked lovely as always. Her dark hair was pulled back and secured with a clip or something in the back. With her hair that way, it showed off her face so well. And her neck. I loved looking at the whiteness of her neck. It made me right hungry. She wore sockless boat shoes, tailored almost knee-length shorts and a green cotton golf shirt that accented her pert little breasts.

Martin opened the screen door and came to stand by his mother, scowling at me.

"You look great," I said. "You too, Martin. I know you're happy to see me."

The scowl left his face, replaced by the vague beginnings of a shy smile.

"Want to take a little ride?" I said.

"We're ready," Elly said, and took Martin's hand and approached my car. Moving around to the other side, I opened the passenger door and the door behind it. I gave Elly a discreet kiss on the cheek and put my hand on top of Martin's head in sort of a pat.

Elly started getting Martin into the backseat. "How

come I never get to sit in the front?" Martin said.

"You sometimes sit in the front when Mr. Weaver takes you and Lauren to play Putt-Putt," Elly said, buckling Martin into the back seatbelt.

We were on our way. That far out of Manteo and heading toward the Mann's Harbor Bridge rather than the newer Virginia Dare Memorial Bridge, the traffic was light. Crossing the Croatan Sound, the water reflected the virtually cloudless blue sky and took on some of the bluish tint. The water was smooth and with an almost metallic cast to it. A lone fisherman had pulled his powerboat close to the bridge's pilings. We could see the graceful arch of the Virginia Dare bridge off to our left appearing to stretch from horizon to horizon.

We exited the bridge and entered Mann's Harbor. We turned left, then right, passing Stan's Market, and continued up the highway a couple of miles. I slowed just beyond a gentle curve. I pointed to the woods on the right. "See that little road? That's the one that leads into the Bear Woman's property."

Elly leaned toward her window. "Hardly a road at all."

Checking the rearview mirror, I slowed even more. I lowered my window a few inches. I could smell the sun on the pine trees. "I expect Balls and Odell are back in there somewhere interviewing the neighbors."

Elly glanced over at me. "You wish you were back there with them." It was a statement, not a question.

"I'm happy right where I am . . . with you and Martin."

"Um-huh."

Martin, hearing his name became more alert. "We getting some ice cream? I'm hungry."

"Yes, Martin," I said. "In just a few minutes."

A half a mile or so farther down the highway, another road—and more of a real road—turned off to the right. "Down that road, I presume, is where the neighbors live," I said, more to myself than to Elly. I slowed even more.

"Are you going down there?"

"No, just sort of checking it out," I said.

Elly gave a short laugh. "You're just squirming to get involved with it, aren't you?"

I smiled and picked up my speed. A short distance ahead there was a turnoff at a white wooden community center with a circular drive. I pulled in there and turned back the way we had come.

Elly glanced at the woods. "You know, I'd heard about the Bear Woman since I guess I was a teenager. I always thought it was just one of the—what?—eccentric or exotic things about this area. I don't think I even thought it was unusual." She gave another short chuckle and glanced at my profile. "You know, like doesn't everyone have a Bear Woman living in their community?" Then she got quiet. I stole a quick peek at her face. She stared straight ahead. "It's kind of sad, I think, but all those years I'd heard of the Bear Woman, I never knew her name until this happened— Estelle."

"I understand," I said. "As I went through her trailer and saw her books and then read through her papers, it was only then that she became a real person to me, and not just—I hate to say it—not just an oddity."

Elly nodded.

"I'm starving," Martin said.

"Okay. We're heading back to Stan's Market—and ice cream if your mama agrees."

"Mother . . . please."

"I agree," Elly said.

"Oh boy!"

In a few minutes, we pulled into the partly paved apron at Stan's Market. To our right the parking area was gravel. Martin struggled to get unhooked from his seatbelt. Elly quickly got out to help him. We walked toward the entrance, with Martin leading the way, tugging at his mother's hand to move her along.

Three young children, maybe a year or two older than Martin, stood outside just beyond the front door and eyed us without speaking. They concentrated on Martin. He didn't act like he had even seen them. Two were boys, one white the other black, and a little white girl who was maybe the oldest, although they were all pretty close to the same age. They were dressed rather scruffily in shorts, T-shirts, and flip-flops. The T-shirts, and probably the shorts, could have benefitted from a washing machine. A little scrubbing wouldn't have hurt their faces either.

Martin hurried straight to the ice cream freezer.

Stan, coming from the back of the market to the front, smiled at us and nodded. "Howdy." He was in a short-sleeve faded green shirt and khaki pants. Work shoes with thick soles, good for standing on your feet much of the day. A middle-aged woman with a full head of very black hair—except for the gray showing at the part—was at the cash register behind the counter. She nodded.

Elly went to the ice cream freezer to help Martin with his selection—and to reach into the freezer, which was beyond Martin's arm length. "A Nutty-Buddy," he said, rubbing his palms together. Couldn't wait.

I spoke to Stan. Just passing the mundane back and forth. I reached for my wallet as Elly came forward with Martin and the Nutty-Buddy, already being unwrapped.

"I'll get this," she said.

"No, no. I've got it." I went to the woman with the very black hair.

Elly came up and lightly touched my arm. She canted her head toward the front door. "Those children out there." There was a concern in her eyes. "I just can't have Martin eating this ice cream and . . . and they look so . . . I don't know, Harrison."

"Yes," I said softly. I paid for Martin's ice cream and then approached Stan, who was restacking small cans of peaches.

Elly kept Martin inside, showing him some of the small toys in a bin to the left of the door. The three children stood just outside the door, more or less where they were when we came in.

"Stan?"

He looked up and smiled. "Yeah?"

"Those three little kids outside. You think it'd be all right if I bought them ice cream, too?"

Stan chuckled, his belly moving up and down over his low-slung belt. "Those little scalawags. I don't know how they can time it, but they always seem to know when a—I started to say 'soft touch' comes along—but I'll change that to Good Samaritan." He shook his big head and kept on smiling. "Sure. They'd be tickled to death."

Elly heard the conversation and she said, "Thank you. I'll ask them." She stepped outside and bent over a bit talking to the children. They grinned and followed her back inside. She steered them to the ice cream freezer, as if she had to. They knew exactly where it was.

The little girl selected an ice cream sandwich; one boy got a Nutty-Buddy and the white boy picked up a Popsicle, put it down and picked up another one.

"Just one apiece," Elly said, using something of a teacher's voice.

The boy shrugged and selected a chocolate covered ice cream on a stick.

The little girl said, "Thank you," and the boys mumbled something, unwrapping their stash.

"Put the paper in that trash can," Elly said, and they obliged.

Then they went back outside, already adding some of the ice cream drippings to their face and shirts. One of the boys wiped his sticky hand on his trousers. Martin kept an eye on them through the window before turning his attention back to the toys and novelties displayed in the case.

As I paid for the extra ice cream, Stan strolled over,

leaning one elbow on the counter. He chuckled, "Between you and Devon Sasser those kids make out pretty good."

"Yes," I said. "I know Devon. He stop by here often?"

"Yeah, just about every time he comes back through from making his sales calls around the state." He leaned back up and put his hands deep in his pockets. "And those little kids—they live just up the road a piece—can I guess hear that SUV of his coming down the road . . . and here they are."

"He always buy them ice cream?"

"Oh, yeah, or snacks or something every time. He seems right fond of them." He got a sorrowful expression on his big face and shook his head. "Shame about his ex-wife, Estelle, the folks called the Bear Woman."

"Yes, it was," I said. He had my full attention. Elly stood several feet away with Martin, but I knew she was listening to the conversation.

"I just read about it in *The Virginian-Pilot* the other morning. Saw something on TV about it too. She was murdered, huh?"

"Looks that way," I said, rather vaguely.

"You writing about it?" he asked, head cocked, eyeing me.

So much for anonymity. "Oh, I don't know. It's interesting." I leaned against the counter, relaxed, wanted to keep him engaged. "Was she a regular customer here?"

"Oh, yeah. Coming here for years. Not too often, but every week or so." He gave a half-smile. "Bought a few supplies for herself from time to time, but lots of stuff for those damn bears." He shook his head, remembering. "Once in a while I'd give her a real good price on some out of date stuff, like peanut butter and maybe some honey that was getting sugary. For the bears, I know."

"Money? She always have money?"

"Most of the time, yeah. I guess she got some sort of pension or something and then those women what kinda adopted her I think gave her some money from time to time. Sort of a collection."

I nodded. Pretending to turn my attention to what Martin was doing, I said casually, "When was the last time you saw her?"

That sorrowful expression came back full force. "That's a sad thing. She was here just last week. Not more'n a day or so before she was killed." He shook his head. "She'd changed a lot. Looking haggard, you know. Could tell, too, she been wearing the same clothes for quite a spell. Over the years, I saw her change and age—hell, like all of us. But here this last time she looked real wore out. Distracted, too, like something was on her mind."

"That's too bad," I said to fill in a pause, but I wanted him to keep talking.

"As she was leaving, it so happened that Devon, her ex you know, came driving up. They stood out there in the driveway talking a bit. Well, I say talking, but you know how ex-husbands and wives are, looked more like they was arguing than talking. Then she got in that old car of hers and drove away." He raised his eyebrows and turned down his lips. "Guess maybe Devon was kinda upset because he never came in the store. Didn't even buy those little scalawags any ice cream like he usually did. He just drove away." He paused.

"I guess he went back toward the beach," I said, and studied him closely.

"Reckon so. But I got busy and didn't watch anymore." Then he shut down. "I don't want you to think I'm gossiping, you know. But you asked."

"No, sir, Stan. You're not gossiping. Just talking about somebody we're all interested in. A real shame."

"'Tis that," he said.

At that moment, an elderly couple shuffled in. The man looked as though he had trouble walking and the equally frail-looking woman kept a hand on his elbow. Stan greeted them by name. To me he said, "Good to talk with you, Mr. Weaver. Gotta tend to my friends here."

I thanked him and turned to Elly. She said, "I'm going to get this box of crayons for Martin." She came to the cashier, glancing over at me. "You ready to go?"

"Huh? Oh, yes. Yes." I know I sounded like my mind was a thousand miles away.

Elly gave quick study of my face, and nodded.

Outside, the three little children had disappeared. I opened the car doors for Elly and for Martin and she began buckling him in.

Silently, I circled back around to the driver's door and got in. I knew Elly was watching me. We pulled out of the parking area, checked for traffic, and then headed back toward Roanoke Island.

Finally, Elly asked, "You learned something back there?"

I didn't answer for a beat or two. "Devon Sasser told us he hadn't seen his ex-wife since the first of the year. But apparently he saw her shortly before she was killed, according to Stan."

"Why would Devon lie to you?"

"I don't know. But I need to tell Balls."

Chapter Thirty-Three

After I took Elly and Martin to their home, I drove back toward Kill Devil Hills. I knew I had not been very good company after we left Stan's Market. I guess I get that way when I'm thinking and mulling something over in my mind. It's like I sort of fade away from those around me. At least that's what they tell me. But Elly, bless her heart, has gotten so she understands.

I wanted to call Balls, but first I wanted to do some thinking on my own. There was that statement that Stan made about how much Estelle had changed, how haggard and distracted she seemed; and I wanted to go over that last bit of poetry she had written, the one in which she was obviously deeply depressed about something, something that haunted her.

Upstairs at my house I barely spoke to Janey, who chirped in vain trying to get my attention. I sat at my dinette table of a desk and slipped out that one piece of paper on which I had copied that one poem of Estelle's. I like poetry but I'm not a real good judge of some of the more modern, obscure blank verse; however, any poetry anyone has written I figure has been done with a full load of emotion and feeling, so it should be treated with respect. You owe that to the writer.

I reread her verses and thought about them. Then I studied them again and let my imagination try to capture what it was she was saying. I kept staring at the lines, then looking up out the window, and back at the lines again—the verses that she tacked onto the end of the fragment of the poem by Thomas Bailey Aldrich: *"My mind lets go a thousand things . . ."*

For about the tenth time, I reread her poem:

But my mind won't let go of a deed so horrid
It drives sharp nails into my forehead.
The memory is there, not buried so deep
As the one who 'neath the soil does sleep
Decades so long she does sleep, sleep, sleep
I can no longer let her lie so deep . . .

In a few minutes, as thoughts bounced around in my head, one kept coming to the foreground.

And I called Balls.

"I'm busy," he said.

"Figured you were."

"Odell and I are headed back to talk to the Cummins brothers again."

"They look interesting?"

"The older one's got a lot of anger in him, real rage. He didn't like the Bear Woman, and makes no bones about it. His younger brother's not too swift . . . but he'd do anything the older one would tell him to do. Got a put the fear of God in 'em. Rather get 'em outa that drug business I know they're in than lock 'em up."

I didn't say anything for a beat or two.

So Balls said, "What'd you call me for? Just to bug me?"

"Balls, I've been thinking . . ."

"Well that's a bad sign."

"Really, two things." I wanted to present them to catch his interest. "Elly and Martin and I stopped by Stan's Market this morning, got to talking with Stan. He said Devon Sasser comes by his place frequently and last week he was there at the same time Estelle was there and the two of them stood out in the parking lot for several minutes or so, talking or arguing, maybe."

Balls was quiet. I could hear road noise and figured they were crossing the bridge headed back out to the site. "Interesting," he said, and I could tell he was giving it a lot of thought.

"Yes, interesting because he told us he hadn't seen his ex-wife since the first of the year."

"I remember," he said quietly. Then he said, "What's the other thing? You said there were two."

"Well, Balls, I've been rereading that poem that Estelle wrote . . ."

"I'm trying to track down a killer and you're reading poetry?"

But I could tell he was interested and not at all putting me down. "She was getting more and more distressed about something out there at her place, Balls. And this has occurred to me . . ."

"Okay, let's have it. Another one of your wild imaginations, brought on by sitting around reading poetry."

I had his attention. I knew that. He trusted my instincts, just making a show of riding me. "Okay, Balls, while sitting around reading poetry, it occurred to me that just perhaps— now bear with me, no pun intended—just perhaps Estelle was killed, not in a struggle with her assailant who came upon her and hit her in the head with a shovel—a shovel that has disappeared—but just suppose she was killed not because she just happened to be there burying trash or something—but maybe, Balls, she was killed because she was trying not to bury something but to dig up something that *had* been buried."

His tone was serious. "You think there might be something buried there?"

"Yes."

"What?"

"Something bad."

He was quiet for so long I wasn't sure he was still there. The road noise had become quieter. They were across the bridge, headed toward East Lake. "Odell and I gotta go lean on those Cummins brothers again. Be getting late when we get through." He paused again. "If something's buried there, it ain't going no where before tomorrow morning. We'll check it out then. Odell and me."

"I want to come too."

"Christ. Okay. Your idea anyway. If it doesn't pan out . . ."

"I know. You can give me a hard time."

"Sunday morning. Shit. Lorraine wants me to go to church with her . . ."

I could picture him sitting in the passenger seat of the cruiser, Odell driving, and Balls shaking his head in frustration. "Maybe it's time for me to retire."

He was making that comment more frequently lately. Maybe he believed it.

"I'm going home tonight after we finish with the Cummins. One night at home anyway. I'll pick you up at nine in the morning . . . with your shovel. We'll stop at Dunkin' Donuts and grab a coffee and goodies. Head on out, pick up Odell if he's crazy enough to want to go."

I heard Odell: "Don't want to miss it," he said loudly. But I wondered if there wasn't a touch of dread or apprehension in his voice.

Before he ended the call, Balls said, "Wonder why good ol' Devon Sasser lied to us about the last time he saw Estelle."

"Maybe because that wasn't the last time he saw her," I said.

Chapter Thirty-Four

At nine Sunday morning, I stood outside at the end of the carport in the sun, a long-handled shovel propped beside me against one of the posts. As Balls drove up, I grabbed the shovel and leaned on it like in a Gothic painting. Just for show.

He shook his head. "You're not putting that damn thing in my nice Thunderbird. Won't fit anyway. Odell will have a couple."

"I know," I said, grinning. "And good morning to you, Balls."

"Don't know why I go along with your wild ideas," he grumbled as we drove away.

I know why, though. He doesn't think it is such a wild idea and besides, he has very little else to check out, other than the Cummins brothers and one or two other nearby neighbors.

We headed down toward the Dunkin' Donuts without saying anything. He seemed to be lost in thoughts of his own. "How's Lorraine?" I asked.

He pursed his lips and gave a tiny shake of his head. "Not too good, Weav. Really depressed." More of a shake of his head. "I need to spend more time with her, I guess. Be more attentive or something."

I was quiet. We pulled into the parking area at Dunkin' Donuts and sat there a moment. He didn't cut the engine.

"Balls," I said, "I guess we all feel that way when we

think about it. Spending more time with those we love. Being attentive." Now I shook my head sadly, remembering. "When my mother died, my father stood there by her coffin and said, 'I should have kissed her more.'"

He looked at me and the expression on my face.

"Okay," he said, his voice full and sounding louder than we had been talking. "I'll take two of those chocolate numbers with cream filling and a cup of coffee, lots of sugar."

The old Balls was back.

"Got it," I said, just as jovially, and I slipped out of the passenger door and went inside.

We tried to eat while he drove toward Manteo. It was a bit messy but we didn't get anything on his precious Thunderbird seats.

At the courthouse, we transferred to the Dare County Sheriff's Department vehicle with Odell driving. He looked fresh and wide-awake like he had been up for some time and eaten a good breakfast. His face was closely shaved and a little shiny. "I got the shovels in the back," Odell said. Then, with a touch of false bravado in his voice, he added, "Off on a treasure hunt, huh?"

We drove away from the courthouse and started west toward the Mann's Harbor Bridge.

Odell glanced over his shoulder a moment at me, then eyes back on the road. "I looked over some of the victim's papers again this morning," he said. "I read that last poem of hers—the one you put near the top—a couple of times. It's strange. Really strange. Sort of scary in a way."

"Yes," I said.

Balls stared straight ahead through the windshield. He didn't appear to be focusing his sight on anything, just staring. "The killer took that shovel. We know that. What he did with it, we don't know. Maybe he's still got it. But why would he? Why not wipe it clean and leave it?" He chewed his lip. "We haven't searched the brush and vegetation out there enough." He turned to Odell. "You can get a few men out there to look about, can't you?"

"Yes, sir," Odell said. "Maybe not today but by tomor-row."

It was almost ten when we bumped along the rutty road to the site. The yellow and black crime scene tape looked like it had seen better days. A shaft of sunlight came through the pine trees and touched the roof of the faded green trailer. Her car had a collection of pine needles and a few leaves piled along the hood and windshield.

"A decision will have to be made at some point," Odell said, "as to what happens to this . . ." He waved a hand, tak-ing in the trailer, the old Chevrolet. "I guess the county makes that determination."

"Above our pay grade for the moment," Balls said. "No relatives. Just that ex-husband. Let them sort it out."

"The will she wrote out in her own hand leaves every-thing to the local Nature Conservancy," I said.

"Yeah that's right." Balls chuckled as he got out of the vehicle. "There'll still be a fight about it, if I know folks . . . and I think I do."

Odell opened the back and got out a shovel. There were two of them, and I took one. We were all three dressed cas-ually enough to do some digging.

We carried the two shovels and walked the short dis-tance up the path to the little clearing where Estelle Byerly had been killed. We stood there a minute. Odell and I held our shovels by the handles. Balls looked around. "These are the freshest signs of digging," he said. "Those others back over there by the trailer and behind it, she covered them up."

"Yes, sir," Odell said. "This is where she was killed and I guess the last place she was digging."

I was quiet and a vague sense of dread nagged at me. It was not as bright here in the clearing as I remembered it or as sunny as it was back at the trailer. I glanced up. High thin clouds had muted the sun, casting the ground in dull shadow.

We continued to stand there as if we didn't want to get

started.

"This is probably a waste of time," Balls said. His voice sounded far away.

Odell pushed the blade of his shovel at the edge of earlier marks. "I hope it is," he said softly.

I got on the other side and started digging. After the first three or four inches, the ground became much harder. Digging carefully, I was making a line of short stabs into the dirt from where it appeared the first shovel impressions were made to the end, a distance of about five feet. Even though the high clouds made it a bit cooler, I worked up a sweat quickly. So did Odell. Balls watched, bent forward slightly, his hands in his pockets.

Odell dug opposite me, using the same care. He took off his light windbreaker and tossed it to the side. He wiped his forehead with the sleeve of his brown shirt.

It took several minutes of slow, steady digging to get down about two feet. Odell stopped a moment, holding the handle of his shovel in both hands, not leaning on it, but propped slightly as if he could lean on it. "You see what I see?" he said, his eyes on my face.

I wiped the sweat on my face, too. "Yes," I said. I peered closely at the hole we had going. "The sides. The sides have been formed. Someone dug here before."

I kept thinking of the lines of her poem: ". . . *buried so deep . . . she does sleep, sleep, sleep . . .*"

Odell went to one end and I went to the other. We were five feet across from each other and we started digging at each end, carefully, slowly. A foot or so into the ends, we saw the same thing: the ends were neatly dug.

Balls knelt and studied the hole. It was not that deep yet. Only two feet or so at the deepest. Putting his hands on his knees, Balls eased himself up and pressed his palms into the small of his back. The thin clouds had moved away and the sun was hot on us now. He spoke softly, almost a whisper there in the woods, but his voice was distinct and we had no problem hearing him. "You're right. She wasn't burying something. She was digging something up."

I could see Odell taking shallow but measured breaths. His face was solemn and his jaw muscles moved tensely, steadily.

Balls kept looking at the hole. To Odell he said, "I think maybe we better get some of the forensic guys out here before we dig any more."

"No, sir," Odell said. "I'd like to dig just a little bit more." Perspiration shone on his face, almost sparkling against his skin. "Maybe it's nothing at all." That was said wistfully. But his voice had a slight tremor to it.

"Okay," Balls said. "Be careful and go slow."

We kept our shovels as close to the faint original sides of the hole as possible. We shifted from the ends to the sides, taking our time. We were down now about three feet. Dirt was piled behind us. I paused a moment but Odell, his face somber and determined, kept up a slow, steady pace, gentle scoops at a time.

Then four feet.

My shirt was damp with perspiration.

Now more than four feet and we had a difficult time bending over far enough to dig without stepping into the hole, which was only two and a half to three feet across. The dirt was now mostly clay, with some sand mixed in. It was hard digging.

I had to push down hard with the blade of my shovel.

And I hit something. At first I thought it was a rock. But rocks are a rarity in this coastal area. I knew that.

I stopped digging but gently pushed the shovel down again. The shovel met resistance, and it made a very soft clink. But Odell sensed it or heard it.

Odell had stopped digging and stared intently at my face. I stared back at him.

My voice not quite sounding like my own, I said softly, "There's something down there."

Chapter Thirty-Five

Using the tip of my shovel more like a gentle finger than a digging implement, I slowly, carefully, brushed away an inch or two of dirt. Then another inch. I took a deep breath.

Balls squatted at the edge of the hole, watching intently.

Odell leaned forward.

Then we saw it: a yellowish-white bone. It looked like part of a leg. A small leg. That of a child.

A sound came out of Odell's throat. Impossible to tell whether it was a groan, or a gasp, or an inarticulated word in some sort of tongue of grief. I think he knew. He was certain.

"Stop," Balls commanded. "We've got to get the forensic lab guys here."

Odell's voice came from far away. "All due respect, Agent Twiddy. But I got to know. Just got to."

In the silence that followed, a bird chirped. The sound was loud. It seemed so out of place for a bird to be chirping.

Balls looked at Odell, watching his face. Balls nodded. "Okay, but go very, very carefully." Then as an afterthought, he mumbled, "Take a while for the lab guys to get here anyway." He paused again. "Late this afternoon."

I began again. Moving the dirt by tiny scoops. More of the leg bone became visible.

Odell's breathing was audible.

I moved the tip of my shovel more to the middle and

brushed dirt toward the far end of the hole. My shovel touched something else solid. I removed an inch of dirt.

What looked like a rib became visible.

Odell made that sound in his throat again.

Balls' voice was loud, authoritative. "Hold it," he said. To Odell he said, "Give me the keys to the trailer. I'm getting her broom."

Odell didn't even look at Balls. He reached his hand in his side pocket, extracted the trailer's keys, and with his hand out to the side handed them toward Balls, who took them and hurried back to the trailer.

We both stood immobile until Balls came back in less than a minute with a worn kitchen broom. He came to the hole.

"I'll do it," Odell said.

But Balls passed the broom over to me. "Let Weav," he said quietly.

The straw bristles of the broom bent at an angle from sitting for a long period unused in a corner of the trailer. I turned the broom so the bristles faced outward, more aggressively. I began to half-dig and half-brush with the broom.

They watched me.

I moved the dirt to the sides of the hole. Some of the dirt moved easily. Not all of it. I had to use more pressure from the broom than I wanted to. But I was making progress. Not happy progress, but progress.

"Up that way," Balls said, indicating with the fingers of one hand toward the end where the skull would be—if this was what we thought it was: the skeletal remains of a small body.

Before I'd moved dirt away from the front end of the hole, I uncovered glimpses of more of a rib cage. Just the beginnings of it. Rotted tiny fragments of what looked like cloth clung to pieces of bone.

I wasn't even up to the neck bone when Odell saw it.

A dirt encrusted medallion, affixed to what I took to be a piece of leather throng.

Odell collapsed to his knees at the edge of the hole. He rocked back and forth. "Oh, God," he said. "Oh, God." He moaned, his palms pressed against his thighs. He kept shaking his head and rocking back and forth.

Balls knelt beside Odell and put his arm around his shoulders. He hugged Odell. I'd never seen Balls show that much closeness.

Between racking sobs, Odell said, "It's her. It's her. It's Luanne." He managed to incline his head toward the medallion. I thought for a moment he would reach out and touch it. Maybe he started to but Balls kept his arms around Odell. "That's the medal she got for writing about the Freedmen's Colony." Then fresh sobs, like they were coming from deep, deep inside of him.

"Let's don't uncover any more," Balls said to me. "We'll wait for forensic."

Balls helped Odell stand.

Odell wobbled unsteadily. I watched his face. His cheeks glistened with tears and his shoulders had lost their military firmness. He seemed to have aged. Then slowly, very slowly his face began to change. Anger became visible. Then more anger, a stiffening of his whole body. An explosion of rage in his whole being. "The bastard who took her life . . ."

Balls put his arm around Odell's shoulders again and tried to turn him away from the hole. He succeeded to some extent.

Balls motioned me forward with a slant of his head. I laid my shovel down and came around to Balls and Odell. I put my hand on Odell's elbow. He turned his head to look back at the hole. Balls eased away and pulled out his cell phone. He stepped away a few paces and made a call. To the forensic lab in Elizabeth City, I was sure.

Odell stepped closer to where Luanne's remains were mostly covered. "I want to see more," he said. "Please brush the dirt away."

Balls came back to Odell's side. "No, Odell, you don't

need to see any more. We know who it is. Wait."

"No, sir. I don't want to leave her all covered up. I've got to see."

Balls studied Odell's face. "Okay," he said. "I know you'll be real careful. Could be more evidence, you know."

Odell picked up his shovel, laid it down, and reached for the broom. He began to sweep away the dirt, uncovering more and more of the remains. He pushed the dirt to the side. The small skull became visible. I thought Odell would stop. He took a deep breath and slowly, carefully, continued to use the broom.

In a few minutes, she lay there and we could see her skeleton from her brow to almost her feet. The bones looked intact, like she had been laid out there carefully.

Tears came down Odell's cheeks and he kept swallowing.

Balls phone chirped. He glanced at the display and clicked on. "Good, good," he said. "Here are the directions . . ." And he gave details about how to get here.

He signed off. "We're in luck. Lab folks are just up the road at Coinjock. They'll be here in less than an hour." Then to Odell, he said, "Why don't you come sit in the vehicle, Odell? Rest until they get here."

Odell shook his head. "No, no. I want to stay here," and he knelt beside the hole in what appeared to be a posture of prayer. He bowed his head. Balls and I stepped silently back away from him.

I may have had my head bowed, too.

It seemed like it took forever for the forensic lab guys to get to the site. I heard their big vehicle lumbering over the raggedy road before I saw them. I don't know how we had passed the time, waiting. Odell stayed near the burial pit most of the time. Occasionally he wandered away, only to come back again. He had his voice more under control.

Odell stood by where his sister's bones lay. "I want to know how she was killed."

"We'll see what the M.E. says," Balls said softly. "She may not be able to tell."

The anger was back in Odell's stance, his voice, his face. "She's been here all this time. When did the damn Bear Woman know? From the beginning? Who had access here? Nobody but Devon Sasser and the Bear Woman in the beginning." His eyes narrowed. "Sasser was one of the leaders in the search for Luanne. He kept saying he thought it had to be a tourist, a stranger, and that she had to been thrown in the water." He clenched his fists. "All the time she was buried out here."

The big white crime lab vehicle pulled up. Black lettering on the side said, "Mobile Crime Lab and Forensic." Underneath that in smaller letters it said, "North Carolina State Bureau of Investigation." Two men got out. They were already dressed in what appeared to be HazMat attire—white plastic type suits and gloves. I assumed they hadn't really changed from the previous site. They pulled masks up to partially cover their faces.

"You won't need those," Balls said, touching his face with his fingertips.

They kept them on anyway. They also wore little white covers on their heads. They came toward us and nodded at Balls. They peered down at the hole.

One of the men said, "You haven't disturbed the remains?"

"Just brushed away the dirt," Balls said.

The other man had a camera and he began to take pictures. He took dozens of them. And he took pictures of the surrounding area. The first man knelt beside the hole. He didn't touch anything, just looked intently.

Balls spoke up. "The remains are those of the young sister of Chief Deputy Odell Wright. Right here."

The man looked up at Odell. "Sorry," he said. Then he

said, "She's been here a long, long time."

"Twenty-two years this month," Odell said.

The man nodded. "Nothing obvious from a cursory inspection. Can't see any broken bones, bullet marks on the bones. Of course, we can't tell precisely. Have to get up the remains. Can't see the back of her skull or the bones in the back." He looked at Balls. "We'll take the remains to Greenville, you know."

"Yeah," Balls said. "This is a full Sunday for you guys."

The one with the camera shook his head. "Sure has been. That was a messy one over in Coinjock." Then he seemed to catch himself, as if he sounded insensitive. "No disrespect here, Deputy. None intended."

Odell kept silent.

The man kneeling beside the hole got to his feet. "We might as well get started," he said. "We've got to lift under the remains, load them pretty much intact into a body bag. Some of the dirt, too. Try not to disturb them any more than we have to."

Balls acted as though he wanted to say something to Odell. But he didn't and left him alone. We knew there was no way Odell wasn't going to watch. He kept silent, his jaw muscles tight and flexing every so often. He held his shoulders up and stood straight as the two men began their work.

They brought out a fold-up gurney with a dark rubberized body bag folded atop it. They laid the unzipped body bag beside the hole, and spread it out to receive the bones. They carefully brushed away a bit more of the dirt. The one with the camera took more pictures. He got several close-ups of the medallion. Even the ankles and feet bones were uncovered now, arm bones down by her side. I was surprised there were still bits of cloth, some no larger than a quarter on the bones and under the ribs. I couldn't really tell whether there were tiny remnants of hair on the skull, and I tried not to look too closely.

Expertly, standing on the same side of the hole, they

scooped shovels under the upper torso and head, with the second shovels midway under the breastbones. They made sure they took up about three inches of dirt underneath the bones. They lifted and transferred the load to the opened body bag. But the ankles fell off and the left leg separated at the knee and stayed in the hole. With his gloved hand, the larger of the men knelt and retrieved the bones and more or less put them in place beside the others in the bag. They zipped up the bag and the sound was loud there in the stillness.

Odell turned away and I watched the back of his shoulders. Then he turned back to follow the men as they lifted the body bag onto the gurney. Half-carrying and half-rolling it, they maneuvered the gurney to the rear of the lab truck. I heard the doors close. It sounded loud. A finality. That was the end of the search that had begun twenty-two years ago. And the search had ended there in the woods, not twenty miles from where little Luanne Wright had lived and whistled and been so happy.

There was some sort of form that Balls had to sign after one of the men had written notes on it. Taking off their gear, they got in the lab truck. The driver leaned out his window and spoke to Balls. Something about Greenville and they were sure the M.E. would be in touch. Balls came back to where Odell and I were standing.

With his face close to Balls, Odell said steadily, barely concealed anger in his voice, "We've got to go see Devon Sasser."

"I know, I know," Balls said. "But I've been thinking. No one knows about this except the three of us and the lab guys, and they aren't saying anything. We do want to confront Devon. However, I want to have a search warrant in hand before we do."

"That'll be tomorrow, Agent Twiddy." Odell sounded impatient.

"We'll have to get Judge Nelson to issue a search warrant.

That'll take a little time in the morning." Balls reached out a hand to Odell's arm. "I know you want to move on this, but let's do it right. If it was him, you don't want him walking."

I couldn't be quiet any longer. "What are you going to be looking for at Devon Sasser's?"

Balls glared at me like he'd forgotten I was around. "Whatever we can find. But mostly showing up with papers in our hands, put the fear of God in him." He looked back at Odell. "If he did this, it's probably not the first. There may be souvenirs at his place." He cocked his head to one side. "Maybe the shovel."

"Not the first?" I said trying to sound surprised.

"There've been six other similar cases of young girls disappearing in this half of North Carolina over the past few years. One or two have been found, partially buried. None solved." Balls made a face. "There're probably more, going back at least twenty years. Several in areas where Devon travels." He eyed me. "I talked with your friend Detective Don Quinton in Rocky Mount. He said you'd been in touch."

I should have known. Balls also would have checked all of this out some time back, same as I did.

Odell remained standing by the now-empty hole. Slowly, very slowly, he shook his head. "All these years," he said. "All these years."

It was now getting close to two o'clock. The sun had passed its zenith but it was still strong, slanting down through the pine trees, making them give off their scent. Mechanically and quietly, we gathered up our shovels, windbreakers or outer shirts we had removed while we worked, and headed toward the Dare County vehicle.

Balls said, "I'll drive, Odell."

Odell, walking slowly with his head down, looked up at Balls. "Okay," Odell said. He got in the passenger seat without speaking. He moved like a man who had aged decades himself.

And we drove away from the site.

Chapter Thirty-Six

We rode in silence.

Odell sat hunched forward. When we got on the Mann's Harbor Bridge, he spoke for the first time since we had left the site. "I want to have a real, proper funeral for Luanne," he said. It was spoken softly but we had no problem hearing him. "I just wish Mama was still alive." He paused. "Maybe best she's not, never knowing what happened to Luanne. Maybe holding out a hope forever that Luanne was safe somewhere."

"Maybe so," Balls said.

"Daddy's not really aware of what is going on. But he'll be at the funeral."

Balls parked the sheriff's vehicle at the courthouse. We sat for a moment or two without getting out. Odell turned to Balls. "Let's go get Devon Sasser." He stared hard at Balls.

"Tomorrow, Odell. I'll call the judge tonight at home and see if we can't grease the tracks a bit so we can get there early." He cut the ignition and handed the keys to Odell. "Try to get some rest tonight and we'll hit it tomorrow. He's not going anywhere."

Odell gave a tiny nod of his head as if he understood.

"And remember, Odell. He's our prime suspect. But we don't know absolutely that he's the one."

"He's the one," Odell said. "He's the one."

Balls pursed his lips. "Probably. But we got a do it right."

"Yes, sir," Odell said, and eased out of the passenger side, and Balls and I got out.

Before Odell went into the courthouse, I turned to Balls and said, "You really think the judge will give you a search warrant for Devon's place? Judge is going to want to know what you're searching for."

"I'll get it," Balls said. "Turn on my charm."

I tried a smile as I said it, but I said it nonetheless: "Yes, about as much charm as a charging buffalo."

"I can be charming if I need to be."

Odell stood there listening.

Balls said, "Besides, I've done a bit of checking—you have too—and I'll tell the judge we need to confirm some of Devon's stops in places like Rocky Mount, Fayetteville, Lumberton. Some of the accounts he has there were called on just about the time those other young girls went missing."

I said, "And you know that dark Nissan SUV of his could easily be thought of as a 'fancy Jeep' like the neighbors of hers said."

"Yeah," Balls said.

Odell took a deep breath and entered the side door to the courthouse. Balls and I got in his Thunderbird, prepared to head back up toward my place with Balls going on back to Elizabeth City to see Lorraine.

When we got to my cul-de-sac, I started to get out, putting my hand on the door. But Balls held up one finger and took out his cell phone. "Calling Odell," he said. I wanted to listen.

He got Odell. "You may want to alert Deputy Dorsey or someone else to come with us in the morning . . ." He paused and listened. "I'm pretty sure I can get the warrant." He looked over at me, a grin. "You know how charming I can be." He chuckled at something Odell said. "And see if that new deputy, the woman—Jessica Phillips or whatever her name is . . . the one who came down from Richmond . . . see if she's available." He listened a moment. "She goes by J.R. Phillips? Okay." Then, "I've found it's helpful to have a woman searching inside a house. They're better at it than most males, and they don't make as much of a mess." He listened again. "Yes, I want to show force when we go there. At least two or three vehicles. Maybe a couple of you wearing flak jackets." A pause again. "Naw, naw, that's not overkill. Want to let him know we mean business."

He signed off.

As I was getting out, I said, "I want to go too."

"You just keep your ass away," he said. But he grinned. "Stay busy reading your poetry." He nodded toward my house. "Or practicing that cello."

"It's a bass fiddle, Balls," I said. He knew that.

"Whatever," he said.

But as I opened the door to get out, Balls said, "Reading that poetry you did paid off."

I nodded. That was as much of a compliment as I was going to get from Balls, and I appreciated it.

Upstairs I spoke to Janey and checked her seed supply and water. She was okay. The day was slipping away. Late afternoon was coming on. I wanted to take a shower, slow down my thinking. But I also wanted to talk with Elly, see how everything was going, what she was up to. I began to miss her. Didn't take long before I always began to miss her. She had really become an essential part of my life. Couldn't imagine it without her. That was a little scary. But wonderful too.

I took a long, hot shower and then called Elly. I wanted to be squeaky clean before I talked with her. I smiled to myself over that.

She sounded relaxed when she answered.

"Things sound like they're going smoothly there at your place," I said.

"Yes, they are. It's been a rather quiet day. Martin's actually on the floor now coloring a picture. I think it's for you."

"Always happy to see his artwork."

Then, I could virtually picture her cocking her head to one side before she said, "I've wondered where you've been all day."

I paused several seconds. There was no sense in keeping everything from her.

"Harrison?" she said.

"I've been with Agent Twiddy and Odell Wright," I said.

"Yes?" There was expectation in her voice, and maybe a tinge of apprehension.

"Elly," I said, my voice level and steady, "we found the remains of Luanne Wright, Odell's little sister."

"Oh, my Lord," she breathed, but loud enough her mother heard her. In an aside, Elly said, "It's okay, Mother. I'll tell you later." Then to me, "Where?"

"Buried there at the Bear Woman's place. Estelle Byerly's place. Not far from the trailer. Buried there."

I could hear her breathing. "Twenty years. Buried there twenty years."

"Twenty-two," I said.

"Just . . . just nothing left. I mean, all that long. That's horrible."

"Skeletal remains," I said. "But there was a medallion that Odell recognized right away."

"Oh, poor Odell. How is he holding up?"

"As you can imagine. All sorts of emotions fighting with each other. There's anger, of course. I mean real rage, but there's got to also be some sense of closure. At least he knows. She didn't just disappear."

"I feel so sorry for him."

"Yes, me too. He wants to have a funeral. A proper funeral." A pause. "That was sad when he said that."

She was quiet a moment. I sensed that she made some sort of "tell you later" motion to her mother. "Who? Who?"

Then the obvious surfaced. "You don't think . . . you don't think Estelle did it, do you?"

I was careful how I phrased it. "No one knows for sure, of course. Frankly, I doubt it. So does Balls . . . Agenty Twiddy . . . and Odell." Then I went a step further. "Whether she knew about it, there's no way of knowing. But over the years something had been really beginning to prey on her." A pause again. "I was reading some of her poetry. That's what led us to . . . to go out there and do some digging."

"So horrible," she whispered.

"Yes."

"Then she was killed. Estelle. Was it because . . . ?"

"We don't know, of course."

"*We?*"

"I mean Agent Twiddy."

"Um-huh."

I didn't say anything. I could tell she rolled over in her mind the most obvious.

Then she said, "Twenty-two years ago, Estelle was still married to Devon Sasser. They owned that property together . . ." She let her voice trail off. "He had access."

I remained quiet for a beat or two.

"Harrison?"

"Agent Twiddy wants to have a talk with Devon Sasser." I didn't say anything about the attempt to get a search warrant. Figured it best not to at this stage.

"When?"

"Not today. Tomorrow, I guess."

I could picture her standing there in the hallway just off the living room, holding the phone, with her mother and Martin watching her now. "I don't suppose it'll do any good for me to . . . to try to get you to stay away . . . when he goes to talk with Devon Sasser."

She was right, of course. There was no way I was going to stay away.

Chapter Thirty-Seven

The next morning, Monday, by eight-thirty I was already parked near Devon Sasser's place. I had backed into the driveway of a vacant rental house. I was less than a block from Sasser's. I could see both ways up Bay Drive and had a clear view of Sasser's.

There was no car at Sasser's. Driveway clear. Garage door open and empty.

I glanced at my watch. Only five minutes had elapsed. I might have a long wait; perhaps Balls, despite his charming demeanor, might not get a search warrant. But I figured he would.

I wished I'd brought cup of coffee with me.

I kept waiting, watching the occasional car that went by. No other activity. I tried not to check the time. But after a while I did. Now close to nine o'clock.

Still no sign of Sasser or his vehicle.

One man slowed considerably and eyed me parked there. I raised a hand in greeting. He nodded and kept driving.

At nine-thirty exactly, I began to squirm a bit. Sort of glad I hadn't brought any coffee. I tried not to think about needing to go to the bathroom.

Ten minutes later I saw the vehicles coming up from my right. Three of them. The lead vehicle was that big off-road job with Odell driving and Balls in the passenger seat. I think he noticed me parked there but mostly his eyes appeared to be focusing on Devon Sasser's house.

Following were two Dare County Sheriff's Department sedans. The roof lights were not on; they moved steadily, sedately, no sirens of course. Deputy Dorsey drove one and the relatively new female deputy, J.R. Phillips, brought up the rear.

The three vehicles pulled into Sasser's driveway, the SUV in the middle and the sedans more or less on the grass or dirt to the right and left of it. They all got out slowly, deliberately. Balls had a piece of paper in his hand: the search warrant I was sure. His charm had worked.

I eased my car forward, staying on the edge of the road but near the entrance to Sasser's driveway. I opened the door of my car but stood near the hood.

Balls glared at me and shook his head. I hung back a bit.

Balls and Odell talked quietly. I couldn't hear what they were saying. Deputy Dorsey came to them. He wore a flak jacket that didn't quite reach to his belt. He looked uncomfortable.

Deputy J.R. Phillips joined the trio. Her flak jacket fit trimly. Her brown hair was short, brushed back, shoulders erect, head held high. Serious expression. All business.

I took a few steps toward them, willing myself to be invisible.

A man and a woman had come out of their house two houses up and watched us from their lawn.

To Dorsey, Balls said, "Go tell that couple that this is just routine police business. We're checking on something and for them to go back inside."

"Yes, sir," Dorsey said and moved across the two lawns to the couple.

Balls turned to me. "I thought I told you to keep your ass away."

I shrugged. "I've been here since eight-thirty and haven't seen Sasser. No activity."

Balls nodded and then ignored me.

"Want me to try the front door?" J.R. said. Her voice was husky, serious.

"Yeah," Balls said.

They waited while J.R. went up the six steps to the small front porch and tried the door. She shook her head and came back. "Locked," she said. "Deadbolt."

Balls nodded toward the combination garage and utility room. A door at the back of the utility room led to a few steps to the side of the house, probably the kitchen. "At least that's open," he said, referring to the opened garage door.

"I'll try the door off the garage?" she said.

"Okay," Balls said.

Balls and Odell followed her to the garage. Dorsey came back. I moved forward a bit more.

She shook her head again. "Locked. But it's just the night latch, not a deadbolt."

Balls nodded at the door. He asked, "Can you?"

"I think so," she said, and she reached into the left side pocket of her uniform and pulled out a small leather case. A compact lock-picking kit. She retrieved a tension bar and selected a pick. She went to work, bending close to the doorknob. In less than a minute, the door popped open.

"Good," Balls said. He put one hand into the side pocket of his jacket. "Booties," he said. Steadying himself against the wall of the utility room, he slipped blue plastic booties on each foot. Odell did the same. So did J.R. He also donned latex gloves, as Odell and J.R. did. Balls glanced over at Dorsey, who seemed somewhat at a loss as to what to do next. "Same," Balls said to him, and Dorsey fished around in his pockets, moving his hands past his ill-fitting flak jacket. Balls watched him and then handed him extra booties and latex gloves.

"Want me to go in with you?" Dorsey said.

"You stay here in the garage. Look around," Balls said.

"What do you want me to look for?" Dorsey said.

Balls got that expression on his face—a combination of frustration and resignation. "Anything that looks out of place."

The garage and utility room were as neat as any I'd ever seen. Yard implements, hardware tools, all hung neatly by size from pegboards attached to the walls. Power mower, blower, and weed-whacker, along with a can of gasoline and one of oil parked orderly at the rear to one side. Two large trash receptacles were on the other side, as were two rubberized bins for storage. There was plenty of room in the garage for the SUV and maybe another car as well.

Balls, Odell, and J.R. entered the house. I stood back and waited. Dorsey sighed and wandered into the heart of the garage/utility room, glancing around.

In less than five minutes, Odell appeared back at the steps from the house to the utility room. He motioned to me. I looked at my feet, and he came forward and handed me booties and gloves. "Agent Twiddy would like for you to take a look at the computer in there. Search it, and see if there's anything on it you can retrieve. Anything that might be of interest."

"Sure," I said, and slipped on the booties and the gloves and followed Odell back inside. "Anything of interest, yet?" I asked as we stepped into the kitchen.

"Not yet," Odell said. "But I don't like it." He looked at me. "I'll tell you, Weav, it's like there's evil in this house. Something wrong here. I can smell it."

I didn't say anything. I may have given a slight nod of my head to signal I understood. And I did understand. I've had that same feeling before when I was at a crime scene. Something almost palpable hung over the place. And Odell was convinced we were closing in on what had plagued him all those years. He obviously sensed he was close to getting the bastard. Maybe he was right. Maybe.

We went through the kitchen to an eating area and then a

short hall, with a living room off one side and bedrooms on
the other. Like the garage, the interior of the house was neat
and orderly. Almost compulsively so, I thought. It didn't
look lived in.

We came to the main bedroom. Balls stood near the
doorway watching J.R. as she carefully opened and inspected
drawers in a bedside table. She extracted a folder, flipped
through it and returned it carefully.

She dug a bit deeper in the second drawer. She had her
back to us. She took something out. Magazines. "Hmm, interesting," she said, and showed the magazines to Balls.

There were at least four magazines. I could see enough
of them from where I stood. Mostly young girls, posing nude
and provocatively. Not child porn, but close to it.

Balls shook his head. "This is the sort of thing that gives
pornography a bad name," he said.

Frowning, but at the same time trying to fight a wry
smile at his comment, I studied Balls' face. See if he was being ironic. I settled on dead-serious bitterness. It's just that
the way he said it. Not sure how you give pornography a bad
name.

"Bag 'em," Balls said.

J.R. slipped the magazines into a plastic evidence bag.

Balls shook his head.

J.R. ran her hands under the edge of the mattress, and
then straightened the bedspread. It was a nice, rather muted
brown bedspread. The room did not look like it had been
disturbed at all.

Odell went back in the living room, going carefully over
the furniture, checking the drawers. When J.R. had shown
the magazines to Balls, I watched Odell's reaction. He stood
looking from the hallway. His jaw muscles tensed and he
clenched and unclenched his fists.

To me, as if he realized for the first time that I had come
into the house, Balls said, "Check out the computer if you
can. See what's on it."

The laptop computer and top-of-the line printer were on a small desk in the next bedroom. I went in and tried to get on the Internet. Everything was blocked. Password protected. I couldn't get it to do anything. After a few minutes, I stepped into the kitchen-eating area where the three of them stood. I shook my head. "I suggest taking it to Tim or Quaid at Outer Banks Computer Repair. If anyone can get into it, they can."

"Bag it," Balls said, and J.R. handed me a large evidence bag that was large enough to slip the laptop into. She took the bagged computer and tucked it under her arm with the magazines.

Balls shook his head again. "This about it?" he said. He sounded frustrated. "The judge is gonna want to know what in hell we expected." He puffed out an audible breath of air.

"Where's Devon Sasser, I wonder?" Odell said quietly. "It doesn't even look like he lives here."

"Neat freak," Balls said.

"I think the 'freak' part is right," Odell muttered.

J.R. continued to look around from where we stood. She kept her face blank. All business. Then she wrinkled her brow and stared at a vent near the floor of the hall, right at the corner before entering the kitchen. She stepped toward the vent, bent forward and studied it.

The grate for the vent was held in place with four screws. She knelt and studied it more closely. The paint on the screw heads was worn away and the screw heads showed markings.

"Someone's been going in and out of this vent. A lot of times."

"It's just an air intake vent, isn't it? Why would they?" Balls said.

"Yes, sir," she said. "That's why I want to see."

Odell said, "A screwdriver. There're some small tools in the kitchen drawer."

"I've got a small knife with a screwdriver," I said,

reaching my hand into my pocket.

J.R. shook her head, her short hair staying in place. She started to lay the computer and other evidence bag down on the floor, but then handed them to me. Still kneeling, she reached into her right pocket and pulled out a big, fat, red Swiss Army knife. Really came equipped. I was impressed. She opened the screwdriver tool on the knife, and went to work.

She removed the screws quite easily. They were not in there tight. Carefully, she lifted the grate and placed it beside her knees. With one hand, she reached inside the opening. She obviously felt something. She glanced up at Balls for a quick instant.

"Bingo," she said. Slowly she brought out a brown leatherette folder roughly a little over a foot square. The folder had an unfastened flap over its opening.

She raised the flap and peered inside. A regular manila file folder was inside. She pulled it out.

Pictures.

After a quick glance at the photographs, she handed the file folder to Balls. Odell stood near him, practically shoulder-to-shoulder. I tried not to get too close, but close enough to see.

Eight-by-ten glossy pictures. Of young girls. Balls flipped through the pictures. There were roughly eight of them. Several were of young girls smiling at the camera. An ice cream cone was visible with one of the girls.

But three of the pictures didn't look good. The girl in each of those photographs looked dead. There was a lifelessness. I think I shivered involuntarily.

"Let me see," Odell said.

Balls hesitated. Then handed the folder to Odell. "They're all fairly recent," Balls said.

Odell, his face stony, went through the pictures. I know he was looking for Luanne. More than half of the little girls, appearing to range from seven to nine, were black.

Odell held his head erect and handed the folder back to Balls.

"These girls are going to match pictures of missing and dead girls around the state," Balls said quietly. He handed the folder to J.R. "Bag it," he said. Then he looked straight at J.R. "Good work," he said.

"Yes, sir," she said.

To Odell, Balls spoke steadily, his voice low, a little husky: "We've got enough."

Odell breathed out. "That son-of-a-bitch. Son-of-a-bitch."

"Yeah," Balls said.

We started toward the door to the garage. Phillips put the night latch on as we stepped into the garage. I continued to carry the computer and the evidence bag with the magazines in it.

Deputy Dorsey stood there in the garage, as if he'd been waiting for us to come out. There was a look of triumph on his face. By the handle, he held up a short, older shovel. The blade of it was dark. It didn't look like any of the other pristine tools in the utility room. "I found this hidden behind those storage bins," Dorsey said.

To me it looked like the shovel I'd seen with Estelle at her little garden.

"Good," Balls said. "Bag it. Both ends."

J.R. handed two evidence bags to Dorsey.

I heard Balls say to Odell, "Now we got a go find Devon Sasser."

"Yes, sir," Odell said tightly.

Carrying the laptop, I moved out of the garage to the Dare County SUV and opened the backdoor to put the laptop and magazines on the seat.

Then I heard a vehicle approaching from my right. The driver had slowed. Almost stopped. Then he came forward and pulled in close behind the SUV where I stood.

It was Devon Sasser.

Chapter Thirty-Eight

Devon Sasser sat motionless in his ink-blue SUV. The driver's side window was down.

Balls, standing erect, feet planted apart, spoke forcefully: "Put your hands on the steering wheel, Devon, where we can see them and get out of the car. Do it slowly."

I had moved to one side, out of a direct line between Balls and Devon Sasser.

Sasser leaned toward his open window. "What the hell's going on?"

"Get out of the car, Devon. Slowly. Keep your hands where we can see 'em."

Odell stood in front of me to my right at about three o'clock. He had one hand on the butt of his handgun. Next was Dorsey, appearing frozen in place, holding the shovel. Then, slightly crouched, was J.R. She had one hand at the ready, also. In the other hand, she held the evidence bag with the folder of pictures.

Balls did not have his hand on the big .45 caliber Glock at his belt, but he had pushed back his jacket to display the gun.

Sasser didn't move, except for that little round head of his. I think he took in the shovel Dorsey held and the bagged folder that J.R. grasped in her left hand.

"Get out of the car, Devon," Balls said again.

His hands still not visible, Devon leaned into the driver's door and slowly pushed it open. He unfolded from the seat and put his feet on the ground, one foot at a time. He got out of the car, slowly, standing tall.

His long arms hung to his sides.

And he had a gun in his right hand, down by his thigh. The gun, a pistol of some sort, was pointed at the ground. He lowered his chin slightly, but appeared to take in those standing in a semicircle around him.

Out of the corner of my eye, I saw swift movement from Odell. He had his weapon out, holding it in a shooter's stance with both hands. He had moved slightly more in my direction so that if he fired, his aim would be between the two houses across the street and out to the sound.

J.R. had her weapon out also, holding it steady in her right hand.

Dorsey remained motionless, holding the shovel.

Balls, his voice level and under control, said, "Put down the gun, Devon. We don't need a shootout this morning in your nice neighborhood. And besides, Devon, you make any move and these two deputies will shoot holes in you."

"What the . . ." Devon said. But he didn't finish his sentence. He let it hang.

"You're under arrest, Devon Sasser. You're charged with the unlawful killing of Estelle Byerly Sasser and that of Luanne Wright."

I watched Devon Sasser.

Odell had Devon in his sights.

Sasser said, "That was self-defense with Estelle. She came at me and I had to defend myself." He looked quickly at Odell and back at Balls. "And I didn't kill that little girl. Estelle did. She came after me with a trowel. Tried to stab me and hit the little girl in the neck instead. Killed her dead." He licked his lips, then did it again. "Shit, you shoulda seen her face when she realized what she done."

Barely audible but with a bitterness that cut through the

stillness, Odell said, "You're a lying son of a bitch."

Balls said, "I'm not going to tell you again, Devon. Put down the gun. Do it slowly. On the ground."

"I told Estelle she'd go to prison if she said anything," Sasser said.

Balls's voice came through again, loud and authoritative: "I'm gonna count to three, Devon. Put the gun down or *you're* going down."

His arms still down by his sides, Devon gave the barest nod of his head. It was like for the first time he understood what Balls was saying. One more time he looked around at how he was surrounded. Then he took in, really noticed for the first time, the folder that J.R. held and the shovel that Dorsey held.

Again, giving that tired little nod of his head, a nod of acceptance, Devon Sasser slowly began to bend downward, as if he wanted to get closer to the ground to put down his handgun. He extended the weapon toward the ground.

But with a movement so quick that I barely caught it, he brought the gun up under his chin, pressed the muzzle against the flesh, and fired. It wasn't loud. It was more of a pop.

The left side of his head splattered.

He pitched to the side. His glasses were askew.

I thought Odell was going to fire. He didn't.

Balls stood there with his Glock in his right hand, pointed at Devon Sasser's body. I don't know how he got that weapon out so fast. Slowly he reholstered it. He came up and put two fingers on Devon's neck. Odell came up, and so did J.R.

J.R. was already on her cell phone calling for an ambulance.

Four nearby neighbors stood in the front yards. One woman held a hand to her mouth.

Odell spoke quietly, his voice husky with emotion. "I wanted the son-of-a-bitch to stand trial."

Balls straightened up, took a deep breath. "At least it's done now, Odell. All of it."

Odell stood perfectly still; his face was unreadable. He stared at the body of the man who had abducted his sister. The man responsible for all of that misery. For years and years of it. Slowly, very slowly, Odell began to shake his head, and I saw tears glistening in his eyes.

It was over for him. After two decades, it was finally over.

We were all silent.

Then from blocks away I heard the siren of the emergency vehicle.

Chapter Thirty-Nine

Even late the next day, I had barely calmed down from what had happened at Devon Sasser's. I felt drained.

Determined to move on, I drove over to Elly's. We sat side-by-side on the old-fashioned glider that was suspended by chains from the ceiling of the porch. We weren't even conscious of slowly rocking back and forth. The last of the sun touched the top limbs of the live oak at the edge of her yard. Martin and Mrs. Pedersen were inside watching something on television.

She waited for me to speak, to unload what I knew. Looking first at her, and then out beyond the front yard, I said, "Balls agrees we'll never know some of the details of the whole thing. But there's no question but that Devon Sasser was guilty—not only of killing Estelle and for abducting Luanne, which resulted in her death, but at least six other young girls. Agent Twiddy was quick to have that pretty well pinned down earlier today by having some of those pictures scanned and sent to other police departments. Rocky Mount and others."

Elly held my hand. I sensed she still thought about Luanne Wright. "There's no way of telling, not after all those years, whether Luanne was . . . you know . . . violated or anything."

I shook my head. "Not even the cause of death, precise-

ly. Probably strangled, but no way to tell." I hesitated a moment. "In a young person, the hyoid bone, the little horse-
shoe-shaped bone near the voice box is still so flexible it
doesn't fracture—not like it would in an adult. There was a
nick on the bone, though. Maybe from a knife—or trowel, as
Sasser said." I shook my head. "We'll never be sure."

Elly looked at me. "How do you know these things?
Like that little bone."

"Reading. Asking questions of people who do know." I
gave a short, mirthless chuckle. "Some things I wish I didn't
know."

She nodded. Agreeing.

After I was quiet for a minute or so, I said, "And we'll
never know whether Estelle Byerly had known about Luanne
all these years . . . and whether over the passing years it got
to be too much for her to handle, emotionally." I looked back
at Elly. "That poem of hers, though, indicated to me, she
knew." A sad tone again: "I guess that's the way it is in life,
some things you will never know for sure."

Then I said something that had been playing around in
my mind. "You know, Elly, it seems sort of linked, but little
Luanne wrote about 'The Other Lost Colony' and she was
lost, too."

Elly was quiet a moment. "And, in a way, so was Estelle
Byerly."

Over the next two weeks, a number of the cases of missing
girls around the state were marked as closed. That was with
the help of the pictures J.R. had found in Devon Sasser's
house, plus some incriminating material finally uncovered on
Sasser's laptop.

It also appears that the local Nature Conservancy will,
indeed, inherit the thirty-four acres the Bear Woman wanted
to leave to them. And Sharon McKay, one of the leaders of
the Nature Conservancy and one of the "Good Samaritan"

women who had befriend Estelle over the years, announced plans for a brass plaque affixed atop a small concrete obelisk would be erected there on the property near where the trailer had been. The road leading into the property would also be improved.

No one ever said anything about the bears. But they had to wonder what happened to the human who befriended them, and gave them treats from time to time. In time, I supposed, they would adjust. And I never quit wondering whether that bear she called Cyrano did, indeed, drag her body back to the trailer.

It was three weeks before the formal funeral was held for Luanne Wright. It was a Saturday morning at Odell's family's Methodist Church in Manteo. There was quite a turnout. Elly, dressed in the dark blue silk dress she has, came with me. I actually wore a suit and tie. First tie I had put on in a year or more. I picked her up at ten and we drove to the church. A number of cars were already there when we arrived.

Inside, we sat more than halfway toward the front. Luanne's beautiful casket, a polished wood of some sort with brass fittings and grips, rested up front on a raised platform near the pulpit.

Odell and his father sat on the front row, directly behind the casket. Odell was in full uniform, shoulders erect and looking splendid. His father, a slightly smaller man, sat motionless beside Odell, staring blankly ahead. As Odell had indicated, his father was not that aware of everything going on around him. But he was still a handsome man. Odell had inherited his somewhat aquiline nose and high forehead. I studied the father's face: Etched there was dignity, honor, courage. And yes, pride and suffering too.

Closer to the front on the left side, Balls sat by himself. He wore a jacket and tie that looked like it was about to choke him. "Want to go over there?" Elly whispered.

The service was about to start. "We'll catch up with him

afterwards," I said, leaning in close to Elly. I could smell her shampoo.

Over on the right side, were Sheriff Eugene Albright and Mabel. Full dress uniform for the sheriff. Deputy Dorsey was there, too, as was Deputy J.R. Phillips. A large number of locals, a mixture of white and black faces. Yes, a good turnout. As well it should be.

After the service, Elly and I didn't follow the procession to the cemetery. Neither did Balls.

The three of us stood in front of the church. Balls took Elly's hand in a light greeting and let it go. He shook his head. "Not always the happiest times," he said, "but at least now Odell can put this whole business away. It's done."

"Yes," I said.

Elly looked at Balls. "How is Lorraine? Give her my best. Please."

"Thanks," Balls said. Then he seemed to brighten a bit. "Actually, she's doing better." He grinned at both of us in turn. "She's busy researching a trip to Paris in September— and she expects you two to join us." He shook his head, still smiling. "She's on the Internet all the time, planning where we'll eat, what we'll see."

"We're looking forward to it, too," I said. Elly smiled an agreement.

Balls loosened his tie. He looked more comfortable. "She's found a nice apartment. Left Bank." Then that big grin of his coming back full force. Aimed at the two of us. "She's looking forward to being a chaperone again. Keep Miss Elly here out of your clutches, Weav."

Elly gave Balls a mischievous smile. "Tell her good luck with that."

Balls headed on back to Elizabeth City and Elly and I drove in the warm sunshine the short distance back to her little house.

And to a good, peaceful life, once again.